MEET THE...FORTUNES?

Fortune (?) of the Month: Ben Robinson. Ben Fortune?

Age: 33

Vital statistics: Six foot two, eyes of blue, and nerves of steel. You don't want to get in his way.

Claim to Fame: He is COO of Robinson Tech—and quite possibly a legitimate heir to the Fortune dynasty.

Romantic prospects: He could have almost any woman he wants...except the one he wants.

"I knew Ella would make the perfect assistant, even when she was mixing lousy drinks at Kate Fortune's birthday party. Ella is bright, sensitive and discreet. She's also gorgeous and sweet and all wrong for me. I am a work-obsessed, bottom-line man—and I'm selfish. Maybe too selfish to walk away, even when I know I should..."

THE FORTUNES OF TEXAS:
ALL FORTUNE'S CHILDREN—
Money. Family. Cowboys. Meet the Austin Fortunes!

Dear Reader,

My family recently rejoiced in the birth of our first grandchild. He is a wonderful, albeit constant, reminder of just how quickly time flies.

And here, in the Special Edition family, we're celebrating another reminder of how quickly time flies...the twentieth anniversary of the Fortune family. I never stop counting my blessings that I'm fortunate enough to be part of the Special Edition "crew," as well as having had the opportunity to be part of several of the Fortune family series. And I feel particularly blessed to lead off this twentieth anniversary celebration with *Fortune's Secret Heir*.

Ben is a man used to success. He was born into it and he's confident in growing that success. But that's on the business front. When it comes to personal matters—families in particular—he's almost a babe in the woods. Now he's learned his heritage is broader than he'd ever dreamed, and he's going to lead his brothers and sisters into successfully following that heritage—whether they're in agreement or not. Will all of that take a backseat when he meets a certain young woman named Ella who has had no success so far in business, but a lot of heart—most particularly when it does come to families?

Settle in and find out. I hope you'll have as much fun with them as I did. Then keep checking back for the next five books, written by authors with whom I'm honored to share this Fortune family world. I promise you...the time will fly!

Best wishes and happy reading,

Allison

Fortune's Secret Heir

Allison Leigh

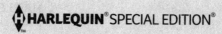

HARLEQUIN® SPECIAL EDITION®

Special thanks and acknowledgment to Allison Leigh
for her contribution to the
Fortunes of Texas: All Fortune's Children continuity.

ISBN-13: 978-0-373-65931-9

Fortune's Secret Heir

Copyright © 2015 by Harlequin Books S.A.

Recycling programs
for this product may
not exist in your area.

Printed in U.S.A.

www.Harlequin.com

Allison Leigh, a frequent name on bestseller lists, claims her high point as a writer is hearing from readers that they laughed, cried or lost sleep while reading her books. She credits her family with great patience for the time she's parked at her computer, and for blessing her with the kind of love she wants her readers to share with the characters living in the pages of her books. Contact her at allisonleigh.com.

Books by Allison Leigh

Harlequin Special Edition

Return to the Double C

One Night in Weaver...
A Weaver Christmas Gift
A Weaver Beginning
A Weaver Vow
A Weaver Proposal
Courtney's Baby Plan
The Rancher's Dance

Montana Mavericks: 20 Years in the Saddle!

Destined for the Maverick

Men of the Double C

A Weaver Holiday Homecoming
A Weaver Baby
A Weaver Wedding
Wed in Wyoming
Sarah and the Sheriff

The Fortunes of Texas: Welcome to Horseback Hollow

Fortune's Prince

The Fortunes of Texas: Whirlwind Romance

Fortune's Perfect Match

The Fortunes of Texas: Lost and Found

Fortune's Proposal

Visit the Author Profile page at Harlequin.com for more titles.

For handsome young Koda Kole.
Welcome to the world, my love.

A beautiful adventure awaits.

Prologue

A strong arm came around her from behind, sliding comfortingly and familiarly around her waist. "Are you sure about this, sweetheart?"

She smoothed her hand over his and the charms on her bracelet jangled softly. Also familiar. Also comforting. Seeming to remind her of all that had gone before.

She leaned her head back against her husband's chest and nodded. "Absolutely certain."

She felt, more than heard, his low laugh. "I needn't have asked. When are you ever uncertain?"

Her lips twitched. She pulled his warm hand up to kiss before moving out of his arms. Careful not to disturb any of the wrapped gifts piled high around its base, she stepped close to the massive Christmas tree—nearly fifteen feet of perfectly fresh Fraser fir—and automatically adjusted the hang of one of the glass globes. Custom-made during one of her trips abroad, it was gloriously beautiful. But the angel hanging above the globe that had been handmade by one of her great-grandchildren just a few years ago meant just as much to her. So many memories. Every ornament on the fragrant tree held a memory. A history. And in her family, there was a lot of history.

For a moment—only a moment—a sliver of uncertainty burrowed under her skin. *That* wasn't familiar at all. Whether her plan would be greeted by cheers or jeers when her family soon arrived and she shared it with them, it nevertheless had a purpose. And given everything they'd lived through, accomplished and triumphed over, particularly in the past twenty years, she knew there was no point in hesitation. She'd been on this earth nine decades.

She touched the handmade angel, marveling a little at that very fact.

Definitely no point in hesitation. Not at her age.

So, regardless of their reactions, it was time to act. Time to move forward. It was the right thing for the family. The right thing for the company. If she had any dissenters, they'd soon see things her way.

Uncertainty yanked out by mental tweezers as if the sliver had never been, she continued to the side table, where she'd left the invitations. She didn't bother fanning through the elegantly addressed linen envelopes. She'd already checked them, twice, against her carefully prepared list. She could only imagine the responses they'd elicit when they were opened by their intended recipients.

If she was in the same position as her guests, she wasn't sure *she* would bother to attend a gala if she didn't know its purpose or even the identity of the person who'd issued the invitation. Why should they? But then, everyone was usually intrigued by a little mystery. On that, she was counting. That, and the financial incentive of donations being made to their favorite charities if they intended to attend. And at this point, it was paramount that word not get out. Lord only knew the chaos that could ensue.

She left the stack of invitations untouched and picked up the two plane tickets sitting beside them, then looked over her shoulder at her husband. A day never went by when she didn't take pleasure in the sight of him. So dear. So distinguished. Her other half, though she'd lived two thirds of her lifetime before realizing it. "You with me?"

He gave her a look. "Always."

She smiled fully then. Not just because she couldn't resist the way his eyes crinkled when he gave her a smile like that, but because she heard the sound of a door opening followed by voices and laughter and excited footsteps racing across the marble-floored entry.

After all this time of thinking and preparing, her plan was finally going to be set in motion.

"Well, then, darling—" she set the plane tickets beside the invitations "—Texas, here we come!"

Chapter One

The line of people waiting to get past the security guard was finally dwindling. It had definitely taken long enough.

Ben Robinson stepped into the sphere of golden light bathing one of the stone pillars leading toward the entrance of the house and joined the line, nodding briefly to the man in front of him as he glanced back.

"Long line," the guy said ruefully, waving the ivory invitation in his hand. He was dressed in a tuxedo that sat uneasily on his shoulders. The woman in a cashmere shawl beside him seemed equally nervous about the diamonds circling her neck, considering the way she kept checking them.

"Yes." Ben's black suit was Tom Ford. Not a tux, but not exactly off-the-rack, either. And he *was* comfortable in it. The only difference that mattered between him and the line of guests in front of him was that they all held one of those ivory invitations that allowed them entry to this highly exclusive event.

An invitation he himself did not possess.

The man in front of him hadn't turned his attention forward yet. "Suppose it'll be worth it?"

Ben shrugged. He was counting on it, but the invited man in front of him didn't need to know that. "Guess we'll find out."

"Honey." Diamond Necklace touched her mate's arm excitedly. "That woman getting out of the limo?" She discreetly waved toward the long vehicle that had just stopped nearby in the circular drive fronting the opulent house. "That's Lady Josephine Fortune Chesterfield," she said under her breath. "I'd recognize her anywhere. You know she spends a lot of time in Texas now. Her daughter, Lady Amelia, got married in Horseback Hollow—that's where they opened Cowboy Country last year. Remember? Oh, my goodness, she's here right now! Doesn't she remind you of a young Audrey Hepburn? It's so romantic that she chose a rancher to marry, but she was engaged to an earl. I wonder if her sister, Lady Lucie, is—"

The guy gave Ben a wry look and focused again on his companion, cutting off her excited chatter. "Let me guess. You read all about them in those magazines you love."

"Don't make fun of me, Mr. Smarty Pants," she warned. She waved her hand at the palatial estate and the line of guests still in front of them. "You're worried this whole thing was a recipe for disaster. But I'm more convinced than ever that this is some big deal about the Fortune Foundation. Maybe they're going to open an office in Austin."

"Who sends an invitation like this without saying who they are? And why would the Fortune Foundation keep quiet if this was their doing?" The guy flipped his invitation lightly against her nose, sending Ben a look, as if expecting agreement.

Ben shrugged again. He hadn't seen the actual invitation. But he had damn sure done his research. He, at least, knew who the chef was of this particular dish. And it was not the Fortune Foundation, which was a nonprofit headquartered out of Red Rock, Texas, a few hours away.

The line moved again then, and Necklace didn't entirely succeed in holding back a squeal as she grabbed Smarty Pants's sleeve and pulled him up to the guard, whose suit didn't disguise either the muscles or the sidearm beneath. Ben moved more leisurely, but soon enough he was in front of the guard. With the dwindling line, there was only one now. When Ben had first arrived and begun scoping out the situation in person, there had been three guards at the door.

"Your invitation, sir?"

Everyone had always told Ben he was just like his father. He didn't need times like this to know how damned true that was. Gerald Robinson had nerve to spare. And so did Ben. He smiled smoothly and pulled his Robinson Tech ID from his lapel and held it out with an expectant look.

The guard returned it with one caught halfway between surprise and suspicion. "Uh, Mr. Robinson." He obviously recognized the badge. And Ben's name. "I don't have you on—"

"The list. There hasn't been enough time. When I heard there might be a computer breach between the ranch here and the headquarters in Minnesota—"

The guard paled a little, stealing a quick look at the state-of-the-art Robinson model computer propped on a stand beside him. "Breach?"

Ben clapped the guard reassuringly on the shoulder while returning his company ID back to his lapel pocket with his other hand. "Don't worry, man. I'll have it ironed out in no time." He could feel the guard's tension and smiled confidently, even though he was lying through his teeth. "I know the system is secure. My own people put it in. But you know how your boss is. Never entirely trusting someone outside the network without a few tests slipped in along the way."

It was a calculated and accurate assessment, and almost immediately, the tension Ben felt under his hand eased. Knowing he'd succeeded, he let his hand drop from the guard's shoulder and stepped through the opened doorway into the house, even before the guard waved him along. He wasn't surprised at being passed through.

Whether a result of being Gerald's firstborn or being the chief operating officer of the company his father had founded, there were few people Ben encountered who didn't tend to see things the way he wanted them to.

He bypassed the long table set to one side of the high-ceilinged foyer, where guests were finding their name tags, breaking up the tidy rows in which they'd been arranged, despite the efforts of the two young women dressed in plain black dresses who were clearly assigned the job of assisting.

The tags were fancy. Gold. Preprinted. But even so, they looked wholly prosaic among the proliferation of tuxes and jewels. Nevertheless, he found them handy as he made his way deeper into the palatial house, following the directions provided by even more party attendants. Because the tags assigned faces to names that, up until now, had been only that.

Names.

James Marshall Fortune of JMF Financial out of Atlanta. His older brother, John Michael Fortune, who'd founded the telecommunications giant, FortuneSouth. One of their sisters, Ben knew, was the Lady Josephine whom Diamond Necklace had been so excited to spot. There were power brokers, movers and shakers in attendance, as well as folks like Mr. Smarty Pants and Diamond Necklace, who'd struck him as pretty salt of the earth.

Yet all of them—save the help—had been invited be-

cause in one way or another they were part of the Fortune family.

His lips tightened and he tamped down the resent-
ment that had been seething inside him for longer than he
wanted to think about.

Invited.

But not Ben. And none of his seven siblings, either. He'd
only learned about the party in the first place because he'd
had the family under a microscope ever since his sister
Rachel dropped her little bombshell.

He finally arrived in a soaring room cleared of typical
furniture in favor of round banquet tables draped in heavy
gold silk and topped with crystal and candles. He wound
through the exalted invitees, who'd begun clustering in
small groups of twos and threes around the open areas of
marble floor, and stopped near one of the three bars set
up in the corners of the room. He chose the bar at the far
rear because, from that position, he had a good view of all
entrances into the room.

He'd been intent on gaining access.

Now that he'd done so, he was pretty much flying by
the seat of his pants. He intended to speak to the party's
hostess. One way or another. How he accomplished that…
well, that was yet to be decided.

"Good evening, sir. What can I get you?"

He hadn't been interested in a drink. Just the right spot.
He glanced over his shoulder at the young woman behind
the bar. She was dressed in the same nondescript tailored
black sheath all the other female party attendants wore,
yet he found his attention lingering on her. The display of
bottles on the table behind her slender hips said there was
no limit to what libation a person might desire.

He might as well fit in. There didn't seem to be a guest
there who didn't have a glass in their hands, either ob-
tained from one of the bars or from one of the attendants

circulating through the room with gold trays and crystal flute glasses. "Dry Manhattan."

He caught the quick dismay in her expression before she nodded. "Certainly." She quickly turned to face the array of liquor bottles, her hand hovering but not exactly reaching.

She had auburn hair. And once upon a time he'd had a weakness for redheads.

But no more, he reminded himself. Plus, no matter how her curves filled the dress, she looked like she wasn't even old enough to be serving alcohol, anyway. The dark red tresses were pulled back in a high, youthful ponytail that revealed the pale skin at her nape above the collarless black dress. She had a cluster of faint freckles there that struck him as ridiculously young.

And she was wearing a Mickey Mouse watch.

"Use the Bushmills," he advised. "Two bottles to your right. There. The twenty-one year." Some might consider using that fine a whiskey in a cocktail a waste, but Ben took perverse pleasure in doing so.

The bartender sent him a grateful smile and plucked the bottle from its neighbors, turning back to face him and the bar again. Her cheeks were a little flushed, her guileless blue eyes chagrined. "I don't usually tend bar," she admitted softly. "I was actually supposed to be doing valet tonight but the usual bartender had a family emergency. I've done all sorts of things for the temp agency, but this one is new territory. Please don't hold that against anyone but me."

It had been too long since he'd been amused by anything a female said, redheaded or not, and he leaned his elbow on the bar and watched her slender fingers uncap the bottle, trying not to imagine how their light touch would feel. "Like the host? Is she as terrifying as everyone claims?"

The girl's eyes met his for a millisecond before flitting

away. "I haven't met her, actually. I just meant—" she lifted a shoulder left bare by her dress and the long tail of her ponytail slid behind her back "—you know. The catering company hired for the party."

It was clear as day that she didn't have a clue what to do with the whiskey. He could have taken pity and told her to just pour him a shot and be done with it. Whiskey like that was meant to be sipped, anyway. Perhaps with a drop of water, but nothing else. Or he could have changed his order to a beer; there was a healthy display of good labels on that score, too.

"Wouldn't dream of it," he assured her. He reached across the bar top and picked up a clean pilsner glass. "This'll do to mix it in. Fill it with ice."

Her fingers brushed his as she took the glass and she sucked in her full lower lip, leaning to one side to scoop ice from some hidden source beneath the bar into the glass. He dragged his eyes away from the smooth skin of her throat, revealed when her collar pulled slightly to one side.

"Now a shot of whiskey," he directed when she straightened and looked expectantly at him again. "Half as much of vermouth. Dry."

That bottle she clearly knew.

"Dash of bitters." He pointed and she quickly reached.

"Now stir. Gently," he added, reaching over to guide her hand. Her gaze met his again in a here-and-gone second and the long crystal stirrer she'd snatched up immediately slowed.

He smiled slightly and let go of her hand.

"I use a martini glass, right?"

"Right. Just strain out the ice." He glanced over his shoulder, surveying the room quickly to verify he wasn't missing anything or anyone. When he looked back, she was pouring the last drop into the glass. "And a lemon twist."

She quickly dropped a curl of lemon rind inside the

cocktail and set the glass atop a small napkin in front of him. "My first Manhattan."

He lifted the glass. "Firsts are always memorable."

Her eyes skated over his again and her cheeks went red. He reminded himself that she wasn't responsible for the animosity he'd developed of late to women in general, and he lifted the glass in a silent toast before moving away a few feet. The spot he left was soon filled with more customers, most of whom didn't request anything more complicated than wine. White. Red. An occasional gin and tonic. Even though he found himself lingering, she was more than capable of dealing with the requests.

Pretty soon, that line dwindled, too, and Ben's Manhattan was rapidly becoming a memory. There was a quartet of musicians playing old standards and the small clusters of party guests were migrating, growing larger as more family connections were drawn and discovered.

His lips tightened and he turned away from the sight, his focus colliding with the pretty bartender, who jumped guiltily as if she'd been caught staring.

In appearance and apparent guilelessness, she seemed the antithesis of the women with whom he'd been dealing lately, and he exhaled, giving up the notion of disinterest. He finished off the drink and headed back to the bar.

Her eyes followed the glass when he set it, empty, in front of her. "Would you like another, sir?"

He had a company of people who called him "sir." "Call me Ben."

Her eyes flicked up to his and her lips pressed softly together.

"And no," he answered. "But I'll take a mineral water."

She leaned sideways again and retrieved a small bottle, which she opened and poured the contents into a clean glass. She set it atop a fresh cocktail napkin and began sliding it toward him. "Firsts might be memorable, but I guess they're not always successful."

He wrapped his hand around the highball glass before she could withdraw her hand, and his fingers brushed hers. "The Manhattan was perfect," he assured. "But I'm driving." It was only an excuse. He wanted his head clear for an entirely different purpose.

"The party's expected to last hours."

He leaned his elbow on the bar again. "What else do you know about the party?"

Her gaze flicked past him, then back again. "Nothing, sir."

"Ben," he reminded her.

The corners of her full lips twitched. *"Sir,"* she repeated.

He felt his own lips twitch despite himself. "Name badges tonight seem reserved for guests. What's your name?"

"Ella Thomas."

"How old are you, Ella Thomas?"

Her full lips parted a little in apparent surprise. She had the faintest of spaces between her perfectly white two front teeth. It added a distinct interest to an already interesting face. Her brows were dark slashes above those translucent blue eyes; her nose was a little long and her smile was disproportionately wide.

Interesting. Mesmerizing.

If he'd been interested in being interested, of course.

"We're not really supposed to fraternize with the guests," she was saying.

"No problem." He gestured at his name-tag-free lapel. "Not a guest. On the job." He stuck his hand across the bar toward her. "Ben Robinson. Robinson Tech." It was strange using the name. As recently as a few months ago, the company had still been called Robinson Computers.

Such was progress.

And regardless of the new moniker, Ella's lush lips

parted even more, clearly recognizing both the company name and his.

Without seeming to realize she'd done so, she placed her hand in his. "You're the COO," she said faintly. "My brother was just reading an article about your company in *Wired*. He's a, um, a computer fiend." She seemed to realize he was still clasping her hand and quickly tugged it free.

"And you? What are you a fiend about?"

Her dark lashes dropped and she shook her head, smiling slightly. "Nothing except finishing school."

God help him. "High school?"

At that, she looked up again, a little outraged. "I'm *twenty-three*!" She shook her head. "College, of course."

Still, God help him. He had ten years on her. "What are you studying?"

"Accounting."

"Dry, dry, dry."

"Some might say that about computer technology, too."

"Computers make the world go 'round."

"And that all started out based on two little numbers," she returned immediately. "Zero and one. Both of which have existed long, *long* before computers."

He realized he was smiling. "So what else do you do besides study zeroes and ones, and fill in at the last minute for missing bartenders?"

Her smooth cheeks flushed again, which only made her blue eyes bluer. "Not much. There's just my mom and my brother and me. I pick up as much temp work as I can to pay tuition. It's one of the reasons why it's taking me this long to get my degree. Never enough time or money in the day. I can only manage school part-time."

Ben and his brothers and sisters had been raised with every conceivable advantage. It was the one luxury of being Gerald Robinson's offspring. They'd never once had to worry about earning money to pay tuition. Or anything else, for that matter.

But when it came to other things? Their genius father was predictable in only one thing: being unpredictable.

The latest of which was the reason for Ben's presence at this damned fete of La Queen Fortune's in the first place.

"Are you all right?" Ella was looking at him, her dark brows pulling slightly together.

He nodded and looked away from her to face the rest of the room, where a hum of excitement was suddenly filling the air.

The hostess herself had finally made her appearance.

And even if her identity wasn't a surprise to Ben, it was clear by the whispers flying around the room that it was to all the legitimate guests there.

The pictures he'd seen of her had told him she was small and slim. But in person, dressed in a pale silver suit with diamond jewelry glinting under the light, she seemed even more so. Then she spread her arms and smiled as brilliantly as her jewels, and her commanding voice filled the hall as the music died away.

"Welcome, everyone, to the Silver Spur Ranch and my ninetieth birthday celebration. I am Kate Fortune."

All around Ben, the whispers went up a notch. Someone even gasped.

Kate Fortune.

Billionaire. Head of the internationally successful Fortune Cosmetics.

And, Ben thought bitterly, the self-proclaimed matriarch of the vast and widespread Fortune clan.

"Talk about a walking advertisement for Fortune's Youth Serum," Ella murmured behind him.

On that score, Ella was dead-on. Because even though Kate herself had just confessed her age, she looked a good twenty years younger. Maybe more.

The hostess was still smiling vivaciously. "I cannot express how much I appreciate everyone's willingness to overlook a bit of...vagueness...and join my husband, Sterling, and me here tonight."

Only then did Ben notice the older, distinguished-looking man standing off to one side of the petite powerhouse. He was smiling, but his gaze was unquestionably watchful.

"But as I said, I'm celebrating ninety years on this earth, and I thought it was high time that I do that with *all* of the Fortune family around me. Since so many of you seem to have found your way to Texas, it seemed only sensible that I find my way here, too." She laughed lightly. "And I must admit that is no hardship, since spending January in Austin, Texas, provides a much friendlier climate at this time of year than my home in Minnesota."

Ben's fingers tightened around his glass.

Kate was stepping farther into the room. "Please, everyone. Take a seat." She gestured at the expensively laid-out tables around her, and those who'd still been standing found their way to empty seats.

Ben didn't bother. He hadn't been on the guest list to begin with, so there was no fancily prepared card marking a spot for him.

When the sounds of chair legs scraping on marble finally subsided, Kate clasped her hands in front of her. "That's so much better, isn't it?" Her smile took in everyone with a skill that Ben could almost admire. "It's a regret of mine that there hasn't been more contact among our families over the years." She gestured toward a table to her right. "John Michael, you've no excuse, either," she said lightly. "You own a good portion of the telecommunications in this great country of ours. You, too, could have picked up a phone."

Laughter skittered across the room, though as far as

Ben could tell, John Michael didn't show a helluva lot of humor over it.

And if Kate noticed, she didn't show it as she looked next to her left. "And Lily, darling, it's been much too long since I've seen you. Ryan was still with us, then. Such a tragedy to lose him."

The striking woman Kate was addressing was nodding. "He was a good man," she agreed.

"And I can't tell you how much I've admired the work you've all done with the Fortune Foundation since his death. Ryan's memory truly lives on throughout all of Texas in the foundation's good works. But—" Kate's smile turned humorous "—I know you've also learned what I learned many years ago. That the heart has no age. And you found happiness again with William, just as I found it with my Sterling." Her gaze encompassed the room again. "I could go on and on, but none of you want to sit here and listen to an old woman talk forever. As your invitations indicated, this isn't merely a one-night party. We'll have ample time at the events over the next several days to get to know one another—either again, or for the first time. And I cannot tell you how happy that makes me. Because beyond all of the successes I have seen in my lifetime, I know that *family* is the most important thing there is."

Ben buried his grimace in the glass he lifted to his lips.

"But as my husband and my children would be the first to attest, I don't do anything without reason," Kate continued. "And I want to ensure the success of my legacy for the future generations of this great Fortune family we all share."

She slowly made her way around the tables. "And the first step in that direction is by choosing someone from among *you* to take the helm of part of Fortune Cosmetics." She patted the air soothingly at the shocked eruption that ensued. "It doesn't matter your background," she said. "I don't care if you are Harvard-educated or if you've made your way courtesy of a GED and gutsy determination. If your experience is in a boardroom—" she touched one dark-haired man on the shoulder lightly "—or in a mechanics' shop." She smiled at Mr. Smarty Pants, who looked like he wanted to squirm in his seat. "It's not what you've *done* that will influence my choice, but who you *are*. I'm looking for a particular ingenuity and strength of character, and I *know* I'm going to find that ideal individual within our extended Fortune family." She smiled broadly and spread her arms wide. "It could be any one of you!"

It was too much.

Too...freaking...much.

Ben slammed his glass down on the bar, noticing with one portion of his infuriated mind the concerned look that the pretty bartender gave him.

"Not anyone."

Chapter Two

Every head in the house seemed to swivel toward him.

Ben didn't care. He stared down Kate Fortune, who was giving him a steely look from the middle of the room.

"And who might you be?"

He had steely looks of his own and he was not going to be cowed by anyone's demands, least of all hers. "Benjamin Fortune."

For about a millisecond, the woman appeared shocked. But then the look on her face was wiped out by one of confident authority. "I sincerely doubt that. I would have remembered putting that name on my guest list, since the real Benjamin Fortune was my first husband, may he rest in peace."

"Oh, I am real enough."

Kate waved off Sterling, who—along with the guard Ben had gotten past so easily—had joined her. "My Ben may have had all nature of illegitimate heirs," she said coolly, "but they were identified years ago. So I'll warn you, young man, that I know how to ferret out an imposter."

"Warn away, ma'am," he said flatly. "I'm no imposter. Any more than *Jerome Fortune* was."

Her eyes narrowed. "Jerome died years ago."

It was nothing more than he'd expected. "He's alive and well and living right here in Austin. And if you cared as much as you claim to about *family*, you'd already know that."

"Sweetheart," Sterling suggested firmly, sliding his arm around Kate's narrow waist, "maybe this discussion can wait."

"Of course." Kate's smile widened once more, but the steel in her eyes didn't soften as she looked around at her guests again. "This is a birthday party, after all, and what is a party without food and music and drinks? Please. Carry on!" On cue, the quartet began playing again and waiters bearing trays of food suddenly marched into the room in time to the music.

Ben wasn't interested in food. Or music. He was only interested in having his say with this woman, once and for all.

Nor was Kate distracted from him. She spoke briefly to Sterling, who didn't look particularly happy, before approaching Ben by herself.

"Jerome Fortune," she said when she reached him.

"Yes."

"We'll see." Her smile didn't extend to her eyes, but she regally took Ben's arm and headed out of the room. When Ben happened to glance back toward the bar, it seemed to him that the only person in the room who wasn't watching and whispering was Ella from behind her bar.

When they reached a narrow hallway, Kate spoke again, her voice calm. Maybe even genuinely curious. "How did you get in this evening?"

"Courtesy of your lax security guard."

"Hmm." She gestured at a closed door when they approached it and he pushed it open, following her through to another hallway. The door swung closed behind them, muting the sounds of the party. "I've never been a fan of gate-crashers."

"Then you should've done better due diligence in rounding up all your precious Fortunes when you decided to dangle this whole Fortune Cosmetics deal in front of them," he said evenly.

She stopped next to another closed door and looked up at him, her expression calculating. "Is that what you want, *Benjamin*?" It was clear she didn't believe that was actually his name. "You want a chance at running part of *my* company?"

He laughed abruptly, even though the only bit of humor he'd felt in months had been courtesy of Ella Thomas just a few minutes earlier. "I don't need to run anything of yours," he assured her. "Nor do any others in *my* family. We're not money-grubbing imposters. We have no need of your wealth."

Kate lifted a brow. "For most of my life, people have been trying to get a piece of my wealth by fair means or foul."

His jaw tightened. "Gerald Robinson. Robinson Computers. Robinson Tech. Names mean anything to you?"

She gave him an impatient look. "Everyone in the free world has heard of them. What's that to do with—"

"I'm Ben Robinson. I'm COO of Robinson Tech and Gerald Robinson is my father. And he *is* Jerome Fortune."

"Jerome died in a boating accident."

"And I'm telling you he didn't. After leaving the Fortune family—" or getting kicked out, which Ben considered likely, knowing Gerald the way he did "—my father obviously reinvented himself. Rather well," he added ironically. "Gerald Robinson is a creative visionary who went on to make his own fortune. No pun intended. What possible reason would we have for lying about anything to you?"

"If it isn't money, then what *do* you want?"

Henry.

The name flashed through his mind like quicksilver, too smooth and too rapid to stop.

"Respect. Acknowledgment." His lips twisted.

"If what you say is...accurate—"

Her hesitation made Ben wonder what word she'd originally thought to use. *True?*

"—then why doesn't your father contact me directly? A man of his standing? He certainly could have done so without need of a simple party invitation."

"There was nothing simple about your party invitation."

She inclined her head a few inches, ceding the point. "Why wait all this time to reach out? If he's really Jerome Fortune, why leave his family to grieve his *death* in the first place?" She folded her arms, giving him a chilly, expectant smile.

If he'd had an answer for her, he'd have given it.

But the truth was, he'd only recently learned that "Gerald Robinson" had never really existed. Not since his little sister, Rachel, confronted Gerald with her discovery of his true identity. And for reasons known only to their father, he was insistent on leaving the past buried.

Ben was sick to death of people lying to him, and in this one thing, he would get the truth out. Even if he had to drag the Robinsons into the light kicking and screaming.

"You and I actually do have something in common," he finally said to Kate instead of answering. "We believe in family."

She pursed her lips, studying him. "I'm not going to say I believe you. But I'm curious enough to want to meet your father for myself."

"I can arrange that." His father would have a fit, but Ben would handle it. He'd lie, if he had to, to get Gerald to the meeting.

And that thought just showed again how like his old man he really was.

"Come to the Robinson estate next week." He realized he sounded as autocratic as her. "After your events this weekend have concluded, of course."

Her arms were still crossed and she tapped one finger against her silver sleeve. Then she finally inclined her head. "Make the arrangements. I won't tell you how to get the information to me. Clearly you already know how to reach me." She opened the door beside them and cool night air rushed in. "Now, I'll just say good-night, Mr. Robinson. Because, as you know, I have guests waiting."

Summarily dismissing him, she turned on her heel and walked away.

Ben figured it was only a matter of time before the security guards came to check that he'd exited. But having gotten what he'd come for, he had no reason to stay.

He went out the door and it closed automatically behind him. When he tested it out of curiosity, it was locked.

"Crazy old bat," he muttered under his breath.

But he didn't really believe it.

Kate Fortune was many things. Of that he was certain.

But crazy wasn't one of them.

He looked around, getting his bearings before setting off to his left. It was dark, only a few lights situated here and there to show off some landscape feature. But he soon made his way around the side of the enormous house and to the front, which was not just well lit, but magnificently so. He stopped at the valet and handed over his ticket to a skinny kid in black shirt and trousers.

He tried to imagine Ella dashing off the way this kid

was to retrieve his car, parked somewhere on the vast property. He couldn't quite picture it.

But in his head, he could picture *her* quite clearly.

Not the red hair. That just reminded him of Stephanie. But the faint gap in her toothy smile and the clear light shining from her pretty eyes.

That was all Ella.

A moment later, when the valet returned with his Porsche, Ben got in and drove away.

Ella Thomas checked the address she'd been given by the temp agency against the small black address printed on the side of the tall building. She hadn't made a mistake.

She moistened her lips and stepped back a few paces on the sidewalk to look up again at the narrow, four-story building sandwiched between one of Austin's newer skyscrapers and a decades-old deli. Aside from the doorbell next to the paneled door and a pair of chairs she could see on the narrow, second-floor balcony, there was nothing about the building's exterior to indicate it was a home. The door was a solid slab of dark gray and there were two oversized, frosted windows, through which she could see nothing.

Rosa at the agency had told Ella the personal-assistant job was for a well-to-do, reclusive client. And if things worked out, it could translate into a long-term position.

And that would definitely suit Ella.

Working for the temp agency provided a lot of variety to Ella's days—she'd done everything from dog-walking to bookkeeping—but a more predictable stream of income would definitely be welcome. When she'd first started with the temp agency four years ago, she'd needed the flexibility in her schedule to help her mother care for her brother. But Rory had been doing so well over the past few years that her mother had been able to go back to work full-time.

Elaine kept telling Ella it was time to focus more on her-self and her goals. Finish her degree. Get a steadier job.

A steady job wouldn't have put you in the same room as Ben Robinson.

She shook off the silly thought and swiped her damp palms down the sides of her navy blue skirt. She'd paired it with her usual white blouse, but had left the blazer that matched it at home. She figured an interview for a personal assistant didn't necessitate the whole aspiring-accountant ensemble.

Straightening her shoulders, she stepped across the side-walk and pushed her finger against the buzzer next to the door. The only thing she could hear was the traffic on the busy street behind her. She could only assume that the doorbell was working. At least she hoped.

It wouldn't be the first time she'd been sent out for a job such as this that didn't pan out past the interview stage.

But a moment later, the door swung open to reveal a dour-faced woman with gray hair.

Ella smiled brightly. "I'm Ella Thomas. I was sent by Spare Parts Temporary Agency."

The woman stepped back, opening the door wider. "You're late."

Dismayed, Ella quickly glanced at her watch that told her she was right on time. But she didn't want to start off on the wrong foot, either. "I'm so sorry. My watch must have stopped," she lied, considering the second hand was ticking right along as usual.

"The Mister likes people to be prompt."

The client was a man? "I agree wholeheartedly." The woman had turned and Ella could either stand in the door-way or follow.

She followed, quickly closing the door behind her. The second she did, all sounds of the traffic outside disappeared.

"He's waiting for you in his study."

Trying not to gape at her surroundings, Ella followed the woman out of a foyer that was bigger than Ella's bedroom and around a slanted wall of smoky glass that would have obscured the luxurious living area on the other side from outside view, even if the frosted windows hadn't. She didn't know where to look first. At the amazing collection of art hanging on the roughly textured ivory walls, the stylishly modern furnishings, or the metal staircase hugging one wall that the woman had begun ascending. To Ella, it looked like the stairs were suspended in midair.

Failing miserably on the gaping score, she quickened her step and was glad to realize that while it appeared the steps had no banister, there was one of nearly invisible glass.

"Mister has parking below the building. If you have a car, he'll give you the code to enter." The woman—Ella had no clue if she was a housekeeper or even "Mister's" wife—had reached the top of the stairs and paused long enough for Ella to catch up, before walking past a dining room table that sat ten and heading up another staircase. It was a twin to the first one directly below it; only this time, there were solid walls on both sides.

"I don't have a car," Ella admitted. "I got here by the bus."

The woman gave her a deadpan stare over her shoulder. "No doubt the reason you are late."

Ella's smile slipped a hair, though she managed to keep it in place. "I'll take an earlier bus next time." If there was a next time. Despite the woman's apparent assumption that Ella would get the job, she wasn't going to count her chickens just yet.

Seeming satisfied, though, the other woman nodded her gray head and continued up the stairs. At the top, she turned to her left and gestured toward an opened doorway Ella could see at the far end of the floor. This floor was more casual, but no less luxuriously appointed than the main floor. There was still an eye-popping collection of paintings hanging on the walls—everything from land-scapes and seascapes to still life—but the leather furniture looked more comfortable and lived-in.

"Mister's study?"

The woman nodded and immediately began descend-ing the stairs once more.

Feeling a fresh surge of nervousness, Ella moistened her lips and crossed the thick area rug that covered a good portion of the gleaming wood floor. She stopped in the wide doorway, prepared to knock on the thick doorjamb.

But there was no need.

"Mister" had already spotted her.

"Come on in, Ella," Ben Robinson greeted from behind the desk situated opposite the doorway.

"You!" Had she thought about him so often over the past three days—since that party—that she'd imagined him now?

"Yes, me." He lifted a hand, indicating the leather barrel chair in front of the massive desk. "Have a seat."

The strap of her purse slipped off her shoulder and she grabbed her bag before it fell...and was reminded of the copy of her résumé she'd brought.

Shaking off her sense of surrealism, she entered the study, awkwardly pulling the sheet out of the protective folder she'd crammed inside her purse. The only items on top of his desk were a computer monitor and a small lamp. She set the résumé between them, then twisted her purse strap between her fists and sat in the chair.

He didn't so much as glance at the paper. Instead, he continued watching her with the same blue-eyed inten-sity that had so unnerved her at the party three nights ago.

"I'm sorry I'm late," she said for lack of anything better.

He had an ancient-looking clock hanging on the wall behind him. It reflected the same time as her watch. "You're not late."

"The woman who let me in—" definitely not his wife "—said I was late."

"Mrs. Stone."

Appropriate, Ella thought.

"My housekeeper. She thinks everyone is late unless they arrive fifteen minutes early."

He was still watching her steadily and she had to work hard not to squirm. Instead, she crossed her ankles demurely and twisted the purse strap even tighter. "That explains it, then," she murmured, feeling inane. "I, um, I suppose I'm the last person you expected to see from Spare Parts."

"I specifically asked for you."

She moved her lips, but nothing came out at first. She cleared her throat. "Well…here I am." Warmth started climbing up her throat.

His lips twitched a little. "Yes. Here you are."

She shifted, angling her ankles to the opposite side of the chair. "We barely said two words the other night. Why would you ask for me?"

"More than two words, I think." He turned his chair to one side, but angled his dark head, keeping his gaze on hers. "You told me you'd done all sorts of things for your temp agency. And I need someone who can do all sorts of things."

Ben Robinson was an intensely handsome man. She couldn't be held responsible if her mind sort of short-circuited a little bit at that, could she?

She swallowed hard. "Like what?" She made herself envision walking his dog—if he had one—or picking up his dry cleaning. Simple, prosaic tasks, that even six-foot-plus men with wavy black-brown hair and laser-blue eyes needed.

"Being discreet, for starters."

Her mouth went dry all over again. "About?"

"About what I want you to do for me."

She realized her fingertips were turning blue from the tourniquet her purse strap had become around her hand. "I think maybe you need to be more specific," she said faintly.

"What do you know about Kate Fortune?"

"That she had to have dropped a fortune on that party the other night." She surreptitiously unwound the purse strap and flexed her stiff fingers. "Why?"

He turned his chair to face forward again. "You were there. You heard."

"I heard you say you were Benjamin Fortune."

"And?"

And when she'd gotten home that night, she'd looked up both Ben Robinson and Benjamin Fortune online.

She'd gotten a computer screen full of images of handsome Ben Robinson, either from the cover of some tech magazine or another, or from the gossip pages, of him escorting one beautiful woman after another to some fancy event. "And nothing." Just because she'd wasted precious time fantasizing over those photographs when she should have been studying didn't mean *he* had to know. "Benjamin Fortune was Kate Fortune's husband and he died a long time ago." The here-and-now Ben was clearly waiting for more, and she lifted a shoulder. "And I assume you're related in some way," she offered.

His lips twisted, this time without amusement. "Yes. In some way, I and my seven siblings are."

"Seven!" She couldn't help exclaiming a bit over that and quickly shook her head in apology. "Sorry."

"We are a large family," he admitted. "And, I believe, we are just the tip of the Fortune iceberg."

She shifted again. "Mr. Robinson, I—"

"That's as bad as 'sir.' *Ben.*"

She hesitated.

"If I'm paying your salary, I can tell you to check the 'Mister' at the door with Mrs. Stone."

"And what on earth would I do to earn that salary?" She sounded as bewildered as she felt. "Mr....Ben." His name felt oddly exciting on her lips. "I can't imagine you'd go to a temporary agency like Spare Parts to hire an assistant when you have an entire human resources department at Robinson Computers at your disposal."

"Robinson Tech, now."

"Right," she said faintly. The renaming of the company during the past year had seemed to be a major media event. Television commercials. Radio spots. Magazine ads. There had even been signs on the side of the city buses.

"And I'm looking for a *personal* assistant."

"Whatever. I'm sure there's a line a block long of eager minds willing to pick up your dry cleaning just so they can say they work for a genius like you."

"My father's the genius." He rose from his chair, suddenly looking restless as he paced across the room to the tall window that overlooked the high-rises across the river. He peeled off the jacket of his charcoal suit and dropped it carelessly over the back of one of the four chairs that circled a small table.

The white shirt he wore beneath fit his broad shoulders like it had been made for him.

She dragged her eyes away, mentally rolling her eyes at herself. Well, duh. He undoubtedly had his shirts tailormade.

"I've also come to learn that my father has been less than honest with us." He clasped his hand behind his neck, which pulled the fine white fabric taut against his long, tapered back.

Safe in the knowledge that he was facing out the window and away from her, she puffed her cheeks and blew out a silent breath. The intense man gave the word *gorgeous* new meaning.

"Not only has he kept the fact that he's a Fortune a secret, but I believe he's kept the results of his past indiscretions a secret, too."

He turned suddenly and she schooled her expression into what she hoped was polite interest.

"That's where you come in." He prowled—there just was no other word for the way he moved—back to his desk, but he didn't take the chair. Instead, he hitched his thigh over the front corner of the desk and leaned over his folded arms toward her. "If you're willing, I want you to help me find them."

Dear heaven, he smelled amazing, too. "Find who?"

"Any illegitimate brothers and sisters I might have out there. Half brothers and half sisters, I suppose I should say. Products of my father's frequent and irredeemable infidelities."

His words were finally penetrating the fog caused by his sheer masculinity, and she sat up a little straighter. "I don't understand what you think I can do," she said. "I've done all sorts of things, Mr. Robinson, but I'm hardly equipped to find... I don't know. Missing persons."

"Not missing. But likely as unaware of their true heritage as I and my brothers and sisters have found ourselves." He straightened again and moved around to sit in his chair. "And I told you, it's Ben. Do you dislike the name for some reason?"

She felt herself flush again. "Of course not. But you... you run Robinson Co—Robinson *Tech*, and I'm just—" She broke off. "Why don't you hire an investigator?"

"Because I want to keep this under the radar for now. I don't want any red flags raised. My father won't be pleased once he learns what I'm doing. About a year ago, my sister Rachel discovered that our father—the man we've always known as Gerald Robinson—was actually named Jerome Fortune. At first, he denied it outright. Now, he just refuses to explain what it all means. Why...*when*... he changed his name. His entire identity." His face was grim. "According to the records, Jerome Fortune died in a boating accident. God only knows what else my father's lied about over the years."

"Like having another family?"

"Or two or five. Maybe he's been a regular Johnny Appleseed, spreading his seed all over the world."

She thought about the slight, ninety-year-old hostess of the party the other night. "And Kate Fortune knows him?"

"Maybe. Maybe not. But there was a boatload of legitimate Fortune family members there that night. We should have been part of that."

She couldn't hide her confusion. "Because of that offer she made? About choosing someone to run part of Fortune Cosmetics?"

"I don't give a damn about Fortune Cosmetics," he said flatly. "I've got all the money I'll ever need. I care about the truth. Whatever the reason he put behind the name change, my father is still a Fortune. That makes all of us Fortunes, too. And if there are other sons and daughters of his, I'm damn sure going to find out."

She looked around the posh study. From the floor-to-ceiling bookshelves loaded with what were probably rare first editions, to the million-dollar view out the terraced window. "If you do find any, aren't you worried about them wanting a piece of all this? What if they make a claim on *your* inheritance? On the Robinson name?"

His eyes darkened for a moment. "That's why I want to approach this from a different angle. I *don't* want to attract the liars and cheats who'll be the first in line if word about what I'm doing gets out. I'm not in the mood to deal with gold diggers. Not again. But everyone has a right to know his or her roots. Don't you agree?"

She nodded slowly, uncomfortably curious about the gold diggers with whom he'd already dealt. "I do agree, but I'm not sure how I'm qualified to help you in your search."

"You're intelligent. You're quick on your feet. You're discreet, and there's something about you that makes people want to confide in you. Look how I just did."

She let out a nervous, breathless laugh. "You got all that out of teaching me to mix a Manhattan?"

"I've done some research, too, Ella Thomas." He clasped his hands on top of his desk and leaned forward. "You're at the top of your class. You've never turned down an assignment from Spare Parts."

"Because I can't afford to."

"You were the only one in the room the other night who wasn't listening agog to every single word that Kate Fortune and I exchanged. And I want you."

Before she could get dizzy over that, she reminded herself sternly that he was only referring to hiring her for this unusual quest of his.

"You're putting yourself through college, right?"

She nodded, not trusting herself to speak.

"Then help me track down my family, and I'll make sure you have enough money to pay not only for the rest of your education, but pay off the student loans you already have, as well."

Chapter Three

Ella's eyes went wide as she stared back at Ben and he could already taste success.

"I'm not a charity case."

"I didn't say you were," he said truthfully.

"If my detective skills turn out to be as bad as my bartending skills, you can fire me."

"Your bartending skills were fine."

"And I reserve the right to quit, too, if…um…I decide the job doesn't suit."

"Why wouldn't it suit?"

Her dark lashes fell and her auburn head dipped a little. She had her hair in a ponytail again. And even though there was nothing particularly attractive about the loosely fitted white shirt she wore tucked into a plain blue skirt, he had to remind himself again that she was off-limits. He'd put her there, square and fair, by the very act of employing her, even if it was through a temporary agency.

Ben never mixed business with pleasure. Ever. Especially with someone as young and seemingly wholesome as Ella Thomas. She was white picket fences and babies and happily-ever-afters. And he was anything but.

His mood effectively darkened, he pushed out of his chair again and paced across to the window. He didn't see the view. In his head, he was picturing Henry. The two-year-old boy who, for the better part of the past year, Ben had let himself believe he'd fathered. Finding out that he hadn't during the same time he'd learned his father wasn't who he said he was had been sour icing on a bitter cake.

He pinched the bridge of his nose until Henry's image in his mind faded. "Do we have an agreement or not, Ella?" He turned on his heel to face her.

"I guess you're not interested in reviewing my résumé." She sat forward and retrieved the sheet of ivory paper she'd set on his desk.

He doubted there was anything on it that he hadn't already discovered for himself. He shook his head.

"And if I decline your generous offer?"

"Then I'll figure something else out." He wouldn't want another prospect from Spare Parts, at any rate. His only interest in the temporary agency was the fact that Ella worked for them.

She pulled a manila folder out of her purse and tucked the résumé neatly inside it. Then she stood and seemed to brace herself before she approached him, her hand outstretched. "We have an agreement."

He'd just as soon not touch her, because even though he'd put her out of his reach, he'd still spent too much time over the past few days thinking about touching her all over. But he shook her hand briefly. "You'll work here," he said. "Ordinarily, I'm not here during the day, so that—" he gestured at his desk and the computer there "—will be all yours. You can park under—"

"Mrs. Stone told me," she interrupted quickly. "I don't have a car."

"I'll arrange one for you."

She looked pained. "I'm fine with the bus. And on nice days, I like to ride my bike, anyway."

He wanted to pinch his nose again, because he didn't want to be having lascivious thoughts about college girls who rode bicycles. Instead, he headed toward the stairs. He'd been prepared to have her start immediately, but he obviously needed another night to get his head on straight. "Suit yourself. You can have weekends off. I've already put together my notes and a list of women with whom my father might have been involved." A task that had almost been enough to keep him occupied once he'd learned the truth about Henry. "You can start on that tomorrow, if you're ready."

"Okay." Her footsteps sounded light on the stairs behind him.

"It's a long list," he added grimly.

Her steps slowed. "I'm sorry."

He'd reached the second floor, where the kitchen and formal dining room were situated, and he glanced back at her. "For what?"

She lifted her shoulders in the cheaply fitting blouse. "My father died when I was eight. But I can only imagine how difficult a task this must be for you."

"It's *your* task," he reminded her, deliberately overlooking the compassion in her open gaze. "That's why I've hired you. Mrs. Stone," he barked, and his housekeeper immediately appeared. She'd come with the house, having worked with the prior owners for twenty years. He figured that she tolerated his presence only because she had to, if she didn't want to give up the house.

"Give Ms. Thomas the spare house key." He ignored Ella's surprised start as easily as he ignored Mrs. Stone's emotionless stare. "She'll be working in my office from now on, so make sure she has everything she needs." He looked at Ella. "I have a conference call in a few minutes from Tokyo, so I'll leave you with her."

She gave him a bemused nod, not speaking until he started back up the stairs again. "What do I do if I, you know, make any finds?"

Call me. "Leave a daily report on my desk," he said instead. "Nothing complicated. Just whether you've made any progress."

Her expression cleared, making him wonder if she was relieved. Maybe she wanted to keep as much distance between them as he did. If that was the case, so much the better.

"Daily reports." She nodded and clasped her purse to her narrow waist. Her eyes were sparkling, bluer than the Texas sky, and her wide smile showed off that faint space between her two front teeth. "I can do that."

And he could keep his mind where it belonged.

He nodded once and headed upstairs to his office again, determined to put Ella Thomas out of his head, no matter how difficult a task that would be.

"You're going to work for *the* Ben Robinson?" Ella's brother, Rory, dumped his backpack on the small round kitchen table and eyed her with astonishment. "Robinson Tech, Robinson?" He barely waited for her nod. "You know his father, Gerald Robinson, was the first one to venture into hybrid—"

She lifted her hand, cutting him off before he could launch into another of his technical, mind-numbing descriptions. "I know. Gerald Robinson's brilliant." And according to his son Ben, a philanderer, as well. She finished wrapping the peanut butter sandwich she'd made for Rory's lunch and tucked it in a paper sack, along with an apple and a few sticks of string cheese. "You have enough money to buy your milk for lunch?"

He made a face and shoved the sack into his backpack. "I'm too old to drink milk."

"You're sixteen. You're not too old." She'd made her own sack lunch, too. "At least don't buy soda. Get fruit juice."

"When's Mom gonna switch back to days?"

"She'd tell you to drink fruit juice rather than soda, too." The Thomases' kitchen wasn't overly large. In a matter of three short steps, Ella could reach the sink, the fridge and the stove. And Rory, even as horribly thin as he was, took up a good portion of space. She stepped around him, automatically avoiding knocking into his crutches after a lifetime of practice, and stuck her lunch into the messenger-style bag she used to carry her textbooks. "And I think she's got another month on nights, before she gets to switch back to days." Their mother was a medical technologist working at the hospital, and the only thing regular about her schedule was its irregularity. But the pay was enough to keep a modest roof over their heads, and the medical insurance that came with it was even more crucial, considering Rory's cerebral palsy.

"I hate it when she's gone all night."

Ella rubbed his unruly hair. Unlike her, his dark hair didn't have a hint of red. He looked more like their mother, while she took after their father. "I know, bud."

Typically, he shrugged off any displays of affection from her. In that, he was a pretty normal teenage brother. "So what're you gonna be doing at Robinson Tech? Can you get any good deals on equipment? Maybe you'll even get a new computer. Or their latest phone. Or at least an upgrade on—"

She waved her hand, cutting him off. "Don't get excited. I'm not going to be working at Robinson Tech and there won't be any new stuff. I'm just doing a job for Mr. Robinson. And what do you need with more computer equipment, anyway? Your bedroom barely has room for a bed, you have so many gadgets."

"Software doesn't take up room, and they've got a new OS coming out that's looking really sweet. You could always ask, you know."

She didn't know what an OS was and didn't care. "No, I certainly could not ask. You have everything you need for school? You've got chess club afterward—" She broke off when he rolled his eyes.

"Geez, Ella. I'm not five. And you forget stuff more 'n I ever do," he reminded her.

That was true enough. Beyond him, she could see out the kitchen's lone window that looked out on the street. "Your bus is here." She waited for him to pull on his hooded jacket, then helped him on with his backpack and followed him through the house to the front door. "I don't know how long Mr. Robinson wants me to work today, so if I'm not home to start dinner, Mom's got—"

He was already moving down the ramp that had replaced the three front porch steps years ago, before he'd graduated from his wheelchair. "I know, I know, Ella," he said impatiently. "Lasagna in the freezer. *'Bye* already!"

It was a chilly morning and even though Ella's instinct was to linger and make sure her brother got on the bus all right, she didn't. She waved good morning to their neighbor Bernie, who was fastidiously sweeping nonexistent leaves off his own porch, and went back inside. She turned off the gas fireplace that had been keeping the living room warm, made a mental note to get the Christmas tree undecorated and hauled out of the house—since Christmas had been two weeks ago—and pulled her own jacket out of the closet.

Riding her bicycle to work was a fine idea, and something she'd done many, many times. It was more convenient than the bus, actually, since there was no schedule to worry about. But with rain in the forecast, the bus was more sensible. With her jacket covering her jeans and flannel shirt, she pulled the messenger-bag strap across her shoulder and set out herself for the nearest bus stop, about eight blocks away.

It could have been worse. The Thomases could have lived farther away from the bus line than they did. And with all the walking and bicycling that Ella did every day, she'd never had to particularly worry about indulging in whatever food she wanted.

Genetics probably helped there, too. Elaine was the same height as Ella and slender. And before he'd died, Ella's father had been tall and lanky.

Not unlike Ben Robinson.

She still couldn't believe he'd wanted to hire her.

Frankly, the more she thought about it, the more she considered his quest a little odd. It certainly wasn't a regular occurrence in the world she'd always occupied.

If her father had had extramarital affairs that produced other children, would she have wanted to know?

It wasn't as if Ben didn't have brothers and sisters already. Heavens. He had seven! A twin brother who also worked at Robinson Tech, two other brothers and four sisters. It boggled her mind imagining the chaos eight children would have provided in the Thomas household. It made her smile, just thinking about it.

But then the Robinsons and the Thomases had very little in common, besides both residing in Texas. When she'd indulged her curiosity about Ben on the internet, she'd seen the photographs of the sprawling Robinson estate. Well, photographs of the stone walls and iron gates surrounding it, at least. There'd been a few aerial shots that showed multiple wings and a sparkling pool and a whole lot of trees that hid pretty much everything else from sight.

Certainly there'd been no picture of Ben Robinson sprawled poolside.

She was smiling over that thought, too, when she boarded the bus.

"Looking fine today, missy," the bus driver greeted her.

"Thanks, Del." She swiped her bus pass over the reader. "How's your grandson doing?" The teenager went to the same school as Rory.

"Oh, he's fine. Just fine. His mama and him are hoping to buy their own place soon."

Ella pocketed her pass again, grinning at the driver. "You're not going to know what to do with yourself if they actually move out."

The driver hacked out a laugh and put the bus into motion. "Reckon that's true, missy."

It was early yet, only a few other riders already on the bus, and she chose a seat midway back on the window. The trip to Ben's house would take the better part of an hour, but she didn't have to make any transfers to another route, and that meant she had a good forty-five minutes to study.

Unfortunately, when she pulled out her textbook for her Intro to Taxation course, she seemed incapable of focusing on it. Same way she'd seemed incapable of getting more than an hour of sleep at a stretch the night before.

All because she couldn't get Ben Robinson out of her head.

Finally, she gave up on the textbook and put the heavy tome back in her messenger bag. She had nearly two weeks to go before the class started. Presumably she'd have her infatuated fascination with Ben under control by then. It wasn't as if anything would ever happen between them. He was totally out of her league.

But a girl could daydream, couldn't she?

Staring sightlessly out the window beside her, as the bus pulled up to one stop after another, letting people on and letting people off, that was exactly what she did.

"At least you're not late this time." Mrs. Stone greeted her at the front door again.

Ella almost wanted to ask the woman if she ever smiled but figured the question wouldn't be taken well. So instead, she just offered a "good morning," and followed the house-keeper inside. Even though Mrs. Stone had given Ella a spare key the afternoon before, Ella hadn't been able to summon the nerve to actually use it. Instead, it remained unused on the key chain that held her own house key, tucked safely inside her bag.

Like the day before, the house was quiet as a tomb inside, and she followed Mrs. Stone up to the third-floor study.

"Mister has already left for the office," the housekeeper finally said when she gestured at Ben's empty desk. "I suppose you know what you're supposed to do."

Ella wondered if Mrs. Stone knew what Ella's purpose there was. Not that it mattered. Mrs. Stone had a job to do, the same as Ella did.

She set her messenger bag on the floor behind the desk and tried to act as if she wasn't totally intimidated simply pulling out the leather chair that Ben had occupied the afternoon before.

"Lunch will be at noon," Mrs. Stone intoned. "I'll bring you a tray."

"Oh." Surprised, she gestured toward the admittedly worn bag. "I didn't know. I brought a sandwich."

Mrs. Stone stared. "The Mister said to prepare lunch."

"Which probably beats my PB and J all to pieces."

"PB and J?"

"Never mind. Thank you. Lunch at noon will be great.

But I can come down—" she realized she didn't know where the kitchen was located because she'd never seen it "—or up," she added ruefully, "to the kitchen. I don't need waiting on." The woman was still staring. Not quite a glare but definitely no humor there, either. Maybe she didn't want interlopers in her kitchen. "But, whatever you're used to," she said weakly.

"Mister never has people working in his office," Mrs. Stone said and turned to leave.

Presumably that meant she was delivering a lunch to Ella at noon just as she intended.

Nervously twisting her watch, Ella sat down in the leather chair. It was on casters. Surprisingly old-fashioned for a man who was firmly entrenched in a modern tech world. In fact, the entire study seemed steeped in old-fashioned touches. The clock on the wall behind her looked as if it had come out of an old railway station. The desk itself was gigantic, with warm inlaid wood on the top and worn metal corner braces that reminded her of a steamer trunk.

There was a manila folder sitting on the center of the desktop with her name scrawled on the front. When she hadn't been stalking her new boss online the night before, she'd been reading whatever she could find on how to locate missing people. Not that his siblings—if there were any to begin with—were missing.

She'd decided the hunt wasn't any different than doing a person's genealogy. And these days, genealogy websites abounded.

She flipped open the folder. The notes inside were typed. Neat. Chronological. She had a hard time envisioning Ben preparing them himself. Probably had had a secretary do it.

There were also a couple of sticky notes stuck to the inside of the folder; handwritten in the same slashing style as her name on the front. *That* she had no trouble imagining as Ben's. He'd written the password for his computer network on one. And on the other, a directive to make herself at home and help herself to drinks in the fridge.

She leaned back in the chair and looked around the study. If there was a refrigerator here, it was cleverly hidden. Besides, she had a bottle of water in her messenger bag.

She gingerly opened the center drawer of the desk and was glad to see it contained the computer keyboard and a few pens and pencils. The moment she tapped the keyboard, the sleek monitor on top of the desk leaped to life and she keyed in the password he'd left, opened an internet browser and turned back to read through all of Ben's notes.

That task took longer than she'd expected, because there weren't only notes about Gerald Robinson's history. There were copious notes about the extensive Fortune family and the mysterious, supposedly deceased Jerome Fortune.

By the time she did finish, she decided she needed to make some of her own notes. Reading about Gerald Robinson's life had been fascinating enough that she didn't feel so odd when she began pulling open the drawers of Ben's desk in search of a notepad. When she reached the last of the four drawers, she'd found everything from a bottle of Scotch and two crystal glasses to a single snapshot of a cute blond-haired toddler boy. But no blank paper. Rather than hunt through anything else of his, she retrieved the spiral notebook from her messenger bag that she used for school notes and flipped to a fresh page.

Ben's material chronicled Gerald's life from his founding of Robinson Tech, known until recently as Robinson Computers, his marriage to Charlotte Prendergast and the subsequent births of their children. It covered a lot of years. From the dates Ben had provided, Ella knew that Gerald and Charlotte had been married nearly three and a half decades. She drew out a visual time line of these known dates. On another sheet, she drew, contrastingly, the brief time line of Jerome Fortune's life span. If Gerald was not Jerome, that young man had had a regrettably short life.

She idly traced her pen over Jerome's time line, while studying Gerald's. She hadn't been hired to determine that the two men were one and the same. Ben already believed that they were. There wasn't anything interesting of note on Gerald's time line until he'd founded his computer company. Before that were just the basics. Birth date. The names of his supposed parents—both deceased.

"Lunch."

She nearly jumped out of her skin when Mrs. Stone spoke.

Without asking, the housekeeper carried the tray she held over to the table near the windows. She set out the place setting, a plate with a silver dome covering it and a crystal glass filled with what look like iced tea. When she was done, she tucked the tray under her arm and headed back out the doorway. "I'll collect everything in an hour," she said as she left.

"Yes, ma'am," Ella murmured under her breath. But curiosity as well as hunger pangs propelled her across the room to see what was under the dome. She was relieved to see a flaky croissant brimming with—she filched a tiny bit on her fingertip to taste—chicken salad, a steaming cup of some sort of soup and a glistening fruit tart.

Definitely beat out her poor little peanut butter and jelly sandwich.

Knowing she'd spent more time that morning thinking about the Gerald/Jerome connection than hunting down any of his possible offspring, she carried the food back to the desk and ate while she began methodically searching the whereabouts of the women listed in Ben's notes.

She was able to cross off the first two almost immediately. One had died childless in an automobile accident only a few months after the conference where she and Gerald had met. The other was now a United States senator with an eye toward the presidency, and Ella figured if there were any other children besides the high school–age twins she shared with her husband, the media would have ferreted them out long before now.

She made her notes next to their names and moved on to the third prospect. "You do get around, don't you," she commented and looked up to focus again on the computer monitor.

Ben was standing in the doorway, wearing an immaculate pinstriped suit and gray tie, and for the second time, she nearly jumped out of her skin.

"Who gets around?"

Over the course of the morning, she'd gotten comfortable sitting in his chair, but now she felt nothing but awkwardness and she hopped to her feet. "Sorry about the mess," she muttered, quickly gathering the empty dishes that Mrs. Stone had yet to retrieve, and swiping croissant crumbs off the glorious desk onto the plate.

"What mess?" He rounded the desk from the other side and angled his dark head, studying her handwritten notes. Aside from Gerald's time lines, which had numerous additions and comments jotted here and there, her notes were fairly neat. But nothing like his typed stack.

Rather than standing there, inhaling the intoxicating scent of him, she carried the dishes over to the table. She wondered if his thick, dark hair ever got mussed out of the severe way he combed it back from his face.

"Looks like you've been busy," he said. "Mrs. Stone taking care of you?"

She hovered near the table. "Yes. Lunch was unnecessary, but delicious. Thank you."

"Thank her. She fixed it." He glanced at the computer

monitor, then back at her again. "You've found everything you needed?"

She nodded quickly. "I've already eliminated two women from your list. If it continues this quickly, you're definitely overpaying me for the job."

He picked up her spiral notebook and read what she'd written. "It won't always go that quickly. Nothing involving my father ever does. Where'd the notebook come from?"

"What?"

He lifted the notebook slightly before tossing it on the desk.

"Oh." She gestured at her messenger bag sitting on the floor against the wall behind his desk. "I had it with me."

"Reminds me of my school days," he murmured. He walked over to her and reached out his arm, but only to open one of the built-in cabinets near where she stood. "Plenty of supplies for you to use," he said, and moved away again. "No need to use up your own stuff for school."

"It was just a few pages," she pointed out. But she pulled out a legal pad from the well-stocked shelf behind the cabinet door and closed it again.

"School's not in session for you right now."

"Classes start up again in about a week and a half." She set the legal pad on the desk, but then didn't really know what to do. It was his office. Taking the seat behind his desk while he was there seemed too strange. Instead, she ended up just hovering there beside the desk, folding and unfolding her arms. "I, um, I only have one class right now that'll be on campus. Intro to Taxation. The last class I took was online only."

"Handy."

"Depends. Sometimes things are easier in a classroom. But—" she shrugged and unfolded her arms yet again "—it's what's been working." It was also hard knowing where to focus her attention. If she looked at him, she was very much afraid she might stare. Or drool. The man was *that* handsome. But it was also awkward not looking at him.

God help her. You'd think she'd never been around a guy before. She wasn't a virgin, for heaven's sake. She'd had a few boyfriends. Nobody serious enough to stick around through her busy schedule and the demands of her family. But still…

"Well, looks like you're doing fine. I'll leave you to it."

"Mister!" Mrs. Stone appeared, unable to hide her surprise. "I didn't know you were here. I'll prepare you lunch immediately."

"No. I had a few spare minutes but I'm heading back to the office. Make sure Ella leaves in a few hours." His eyes slid over Ella's face, a sudden glint of amusement in them. "I'm not paying her overtime."

With that, he departed as unexpectedly as he'd appeared.

"He never comes home during the workday." Mrs. Stone glared at Ella as if she was to blame. "I would have had a proper lunch for him prepared."

"I don't think he expected lunch," Ella offered. "It was all delicious, though. Thank you."

Mrs. Stone didn't look soothed. As rocky faced as always, she loaded up her tray with Ella's lunch dishes and strode out of the room. Ella was fairly certain she'd have slammed the door if the doorway had possessed one.

Fortunately, it wasn't Mrs. Stone's opinion about Ella that mattered.

And Ben had said she was doing fine.

Chapter Four

He showed up shortly after lunch the next day, too.

This time, though, Mrs. Stone was prepared.

As if she'd been hovering somewhere, waiting and watching for Ben to "sneak" into his own home, two minutes after he walked into the study, the gray-haired housekeeper appeared with a second lunch tray, which she set next to Ella's on the round table near the windows. "You don't eat enough," she said before striding out of the office once more.

Ella was still sitting at his desk. And if she had perhaps done a little of her own preparing, too, by choosing to wear a green turtleneck and black slacks instead of the jeans and shirt she'd worn the day before, she was the only one who had to know.

Now, Ben gave her a wry look. "If I don't eat it, I'm afraid she might poison me in my sleep or something."

Ella couldn't keep from smiling. "I think she's just trying to be—" she hunted for a suitable word "—nurturing."

"I'm pretty sure she ate her young," he returned, but pulled off his suit jacket—pale gray today—and hung it over the back of the table chair. "You haven't had a chance to eat yours, yet." He gestured at the second dome-covered plate. "Come and keep me company and fill me in on your progress."

Since he'd made a point of telling her he was never at his home office during the day, she figured he was more anxious to make progress on his search than he'd admitted. She'd been there two days so far, and so far, he'd appeared twice. She pushed out of his desk chair and joined him at the little conference table. But thinking of this as an impromptu business meeting was hard, considering the way he rose and pulled out her chair for her before she could do it herself.

She couldn't envision the man doing such a thing during one of his meetings at Robinson Tech. But then they *were* in his home. To her, his manners seemed flawless. He probably treated every female the same way.

She stole a look at him, while he sat back in his own chair across from her, then pulled the cover off her plate. Today, it was seared scallops on a bed of pasta. She'd never had scallops, but she'd watched enough cooking shows to recognize them when she saw them. "Mrs. Stone is quite the cook."

"One of her redeeming qualities." He shook the linen napkin over his lap and watched her over the bite he took. "Cooks like she was trained at le Cordon Bleu."

Ella cut one of the scallops in half and popped it in her mouth. Buttery. Faintly sweet. A bit like shrimp. And altogether pleasant, she was relieved to find, and swallowed. "I may have a line on someone actually," she told him.

The look he gave her was neither one of surprise nor particularly inquisitive, but when he said nothing in response, she quickly continued. "His name is Randy Phillips. His mother is Antonia Bell. She was an intern at Robinson Computers close to thirty years ago. From what I can tell, after she left the company, she moved to Colorado. Then Massachusetts, where she married Ronald Phillips. But that was only fifteen years ago, and Randy would be twenty-eight now. He has the surname, but maybe Ronald isn't Randy's natural father. Thirteen years just seems like a long time to wait to marry the father of one's child."

"Is he in Massachusetts still?"

"I know he graduated with a master's from Cornell, but I haven't been able to find where he's at now." She took a quick sip of her iced tea. "But I will."

His dark head dipped. "Good work. And when you do, you call me immediately."

She tried not to beam too brightly as she focused on her plate. She wound her fork through the creamy linguine. "Have you been to Paris?"

"Of course. Why?"

Of course, he'd been to France. He'd probably been all over the world. "Le Cordon Bleu. It's in Paris, isn't it?"

"There are a lot of locations, I believe." He gave her a vaguely amused look. "I didn't study there with her. She didn't study there, either."

She flushed. She'd only been trying to make conversation. "I know you didn't. You went to Wharton."

His eyebrows rose a little, and she flushed even more. "I noticed the degrees." She gestured at the collection of frames on one wall and was glad that they were there to explain away her knowledge, because she'd originally read about his education on the Robinson Tech website. She knew he'd been recently appointed chief operating officer of the company, that his identical twin brother, Wes, was vice president of R&D there. In fact, from what she could tell, only one of his siblings didn't work at Robinson Tech. Graham. She'd learned that from searching

Ben's family online. Graham was a rancher or something. There wasn't as much information readily available about him as the others.

"What made you want to study accounting?"

"Security," she said immediately. "People will always need accountants."

"Death and taxes?"

"Something like that."

"Security important to you?"

"Yes." She wasn't going to apologize for it. "Isn't it to everyone?"

His lips twisted. "No."

"Have you ever had to worry about it?"

"No."

"Then you don't know, do you?" she pointed out reasonably.

"Just because my family has money doesn't mean we live in an ivory tower. But I know plenty of people without the Robinson resources who don't give a second thought to security."

"Well, not me," she said feelingly. "When my father died, he didn't have life insurance or anything. My mother hadn't worked since before they got married. I can still remember listening to her plead with the electric company to give her two more days to pay the bill before they shut off our power. It was better once she went back to work, but that took a while."

"How did he die?"

"Aneurysm. It was nothing anybody could have predicted." She lifted her hand, showing the old watch. "This was his."

"He wore a Mickey Mouse watch?"

She smiled, the memory sad. "Yup. He was a musician. Played saxophone."

"He must have done it pretty well if your mother didn't have to work."

That wasn't the reason her mother hadn't worked, but she didn't feel like explaining the demands of her brother's health. "He also was a substitute teacher," she said. "Often at my elementary school. Everyone I went to school with loved him, but he definitely wasn't a planner."

"And you are."

"I think I would have been, even if he was an accountant or lawyer or doctor."

"Do you *like* accounting?"

She realized she'd finished her scallops and pasta. Something about the man made her forget everything but him. "I like everything to add up. It's satisfying to me."

"I'm with you on that." He'd finished, too, and he pushed aside his plate, folding his elbows on the table. "What's more important? Security or truth?"

The question surprised her, but she didn't hesitate. "Truth."

"Why?"

"I'm not sure where you're heading, but as important as security is to me, I think if it's based on a lie, it's really not any sort of security at all. Is this about your father having another name?"

"It's more than having another name. He had another life he's never told any of us about. But no. I wasn't thinking of him." He pushed back from the table and she knew that he wasn't going to say what it was he *had* been thinking about. "As pleasant as this has been, if I don't get back to my office, my secretary will have a stroke."

It had been pleasant. More so than she wanted to admit.

She watched him pull on his suit coat. It was such a cliché, wasn't it? Having a crush on your boss.

She got up from the table, as well, and followed him toward the doorway. "I'll leave you a report on what I find out about Randy Phillips."

"Thanks." He gave her a brief smile before striding across what she'd come to think of as his family room and heading down the stairs.

The sudden appearance of Mrs. Stone wiped the bemused smile off her face. The woman must have been behind one of the closed doors that Ella had assumed were closets. And while the woman was odd, Ella doubted she'd been hiding out in one. Maybe the kitchen was behind one of the doors.

Moving out of her way, she returned to Ben's desk. She'd learned the day before not to try assisting the older woman with placing the lunch dishes on her tray. She'd only earned herself a withering glare. But she couldn't let the woman depart again without saying something. "The lunch was delicious, Mrs. Stone. I've never had scallops before, but I thought they were wonderful."

Mrs. Stone made a sound that at least acknowledged she'd heard Ella's words, without divulging whether she appreciated them or not.

The woman sort of reminded Ella of her next-door neighbor, Bernie. It had taken almost ten years of living next door to the sternly silent old man before he'd even returned a wave or a smile. Ella certainly wouldn't have ten years to make progress with Mrs. Stone. She figured the job Ben had hired her to do would take a month.

Tops.

And that limited time was probably a good thing. She wouldn't have a chance to become even more infatuated with the ridiculously handsome man.

She turned back to the computer and picked up her search for Randy Phillips. For good or ill, the increasing popularity of social media definitely helped. While she didn't find a Facebook page for the guy, she did find over four hundred listings for his name on a business-oriented site. She refined her search, cutting down the field as much as she could based on professions relating to his education, and settled in for a lot of reading.

It was nearly six by the time she closed down the computer. She'd made note of three men named Randy Phillips who met the basic requirements and left it on top of the spotless desk with a sticky note on it for Ben saying that she'd continue wading through the remaining Randy Phillipses tomorrow.

Shouldering her messenger bag, she carried her coat with her and headed out of the office. "I'm leaving, Mrs. Stone," she said in a loud voice, feeling a little silly because she didn't know if the woman was behind one of the doors or on another floor entirely. She repeated herself when she got to the second floor, and to the first, still earning no response, before letting herself out the front door. It locked automatically behind her.

The afternoon had grown cloudy and chillier while she'd worked, and she wished her vanity hadn't prompted her to leave her ancient jacket at home that day. Fortunately, she didn't have long to wait for the bus once she walked to the stop, but by the time she got home, she felt chilled to the bone.

Her mother was sitting at the dining room table with Rory, and Ella dumped her messenger bag on the couch. "Smells good in here."

Elaine smiled. "Thank goodness for spaghetti. I kept a plate warm for you in the oven." She started to get up but Ella waved her back.

"I'll get it." She grabbed a sweater from the coat tree by the door and pulled it on before going into the kitchen. She retrieved the warm plate, which felt wonderful against her cold hands, and carried it to the table. "Feels like it might rain out there."

"You should have had your jacket with you." Elaine pushed the basket of garlic bread toward her.

"Did you get any free stuff from Mr. Robinson?"

Ella gave her brother a look. "No. And I told you I'm not asking him. I didn't even expect to see him today."

Elaine's brows rose. "Sounds like you did."

"He stopped by for lunch. Mrs. Stone—she's *so* much like Bernie, Mom, you'd swear they came out of the same mold. Anyway, she fixed scallops and pasta with this really light cream sauce and we ate at the table he has right by the windows in his office. The view he has of the river is spectacular."

"Scallops, hmm?"

Ella nodded, twirling her fork in her spaghetti. "They were really good."

"Puts my plain ol' spaghetti and marinara to shame."

Ella shook her head and popped the fork into her mouth. "Never," she said when she could speak again. Her mom had once told her they had spaghetti so often because it was cheap and fit in the food budget. Happily for Ella and Rory, they loved the stuff and always had.

"Does Mr. Robinson always have lunch at his home?"

"I don't think so. He's just really anxious about the project I'm working on for him." She'd told her mother about it, knowing that Elaine would never breathe a word to anyone. But she didn't want to get into the details in front of Rory. He wouldn't knowingly divulge anyone's private business, but when he got excited about something, he'd been known to blurt out whatever was in his thoughts.

"Are you sure he wasn't just interested in your company?"

She broke a crusty piece of garlic bread in half, avoiding her mother's eyes. "There's no reason why he would be." Just because she was finding herself intensely interested in his? "He runs a multimillion—*billion*—dollar company. I'm a college student. He dates brain surgeons and beauty-pageant winners, for heaven's sake. Trust me. I won't lose my head over working for him. I honestly doubt I'll see that much of him, anyway."

She nodded, convincing herself of that fact as much as she intended to convince her mother.

"So—" she focused on her brother "—how was chess club?"

"Your messages." Ben's secretary set a stack of pink message slips on his desk.

He barely gave them a glance. "Thanks, Bonita." It was almost eight in the evening and the rest of the executive offices had already cleared out. But Bonita had stayed on to take notes from another conference call he'd had with Japan regarding a software-design firm Gerald wanted to acquire. "Sorry you had to stay so late."

Her comfortable, middle-aged face creased wryly. "That's why you pay me the big bucks," she said as she left his office. "See you tomorrow."

"Tomorrow." He started to turn his attention back to the monthly departmental reports he'd been reviewing, but his interest kept wandering. The way it had been wandering ever since he hired Ella Thomas.

He finally shoved the reports aside and reached for the message slips, leafing through them. He'd left two messages for Kate Fortune to arrange her meeting with his father, but so far she'd ignored him. Which was somewhat of a surprise, because he'd believed she'd meant what she said the night of her party.

He wouldn't be put off forever, though. He'd show up on her doorstep again if he had to.

With none of the messages holding anything of import, he set them aside, too, turning instead to look out the wall of windows behind his desk. It was dark, giving him nothing back but his own reflection, and he got up from the desk altogether, grabbing his suit coat on his way out. He strode through the corridors of the business his father had built and took the elevator down to R&D. The lights were on in Wes's office and he stuck his head in long enough to see that his twin had his attention typically buried in his computer. "Want to grab a beer?"

Almost belatedly, Wes looked up. He didn't always wear glasses, but tonight he did, and Ben could see in his brother's distracted eyes that the interruption wasn't particularly welcome. Then Wes pulled off his glasses and tossed them on his desk. "What'd you say?"

Looking at him was almost like looking in a mirror. "Want to grab a beer?" he repeated.

Wes's eyes narrowed slightly before he shook his head. "I'm testing the security on the dating app we're expecting to roll out next month."

Wes might have been pissed off about Ben being chosen as COO over him, but there'd never been a doubt in Ben's mind that research and development was exactly where his brother belonged. If a person could split Gerald's brain into two, Ben had gotten the brashness and business drive. But Wes had gotten the creative and technological brilliance. And fortunately, none of their father's worst characteristics. The ones that Ben was trying to outrun himself.

"I'll leave you to it, then." He thumped his hand on the doorjamb. "Don't work all night. All work and no play make a dull man."

"You'd know," his brother returned, deadpan, and slid his glasses back on his nose. A moment later, he was once again immersed in his work, oblivious to everything around him.

It started raining as Ben drove home, and once again, he found his thoughts turning back to Ella.

Before he thought twice about it, he thumbed his phone.

"Call Ella," he directed, and a moment later, the line was ringing.

She picked up after the second ring.

"If it's still raining in the morning, I'll send a car for you," he said.

Her silent hesitation came through the line loud and clear.

"No argument, Ella."

"Ah. You must be Mr. Robinson," said the voice he quickly realized was *not* Ella's. "This is Elaine Thomas," she said humorously. "Ella's mother."

If anything was to remind him just how damned young Ella was, it was being faced head-on with the fact that she still lived at home. "Mrs. Thomas. I apologize."

"No need for that," she assured him. "I'll get Ella for you."

He pinched the bridge of his nose and slowed at a stoplight as he listened to her call her daughter's name. A moment later, Ella came on, sounding breathless. "Ben?"

He ruthlessly shut down the pleasure brought about just from hearing her say his name. "I'm sending a car for you in the morning if it's still raining."

"Oh. I—" She broke off. "That's very nice of you."

He'd expected an argument. He told himself he was glad she'd saved him the effort. He would have told her he was sending a car for her regardless of the weather, but knew it would never fly. Not with her.

"Did you see my notes on Randy?"

He felt another surge of adrenaline, this one entirely nonsexual. "I haven't been home yet. Did you find him?"

"Not yet, but I'm narrowing the field. Turns out there are a *lot* of Randy Phillipses."

And only one Ella Thomas.

The light turned green and he shot through the intersection as if he could outrun the thought while she told him about her progress. By the time she finished, he was pulling into his parking garage beneath his building. He transferred the call from his car to his cell. "Good work."

He climbed from the Porsche, tucking the phone against his shoulder while he reached back in to grab his briefcase. "I'll take a look at the three names you left." He didn't expect anything to pop for him, but a person never knew. His phone vibrated and he glanced at the display. Finally. Kate Fortune was calling him back.

"Ella? Hold on a sec." He could have just ended the call, but for reasons he didn't examine, he didn't. Not waiting for her response, he switched over to the other call.

"Kate," he greeted.

"Not Kate, I'm afraid," a male voice said. "This is Sterling Foster. My wife insisted I phone."

Judging by Sterling's tone, it was clear he hadn't agreed. "Mr. Foster," he said blandly.

"She's not going to be able to meet with you this week as planned," Sterling said bluntly.

Ben kept his temper under wraps. "I'm sorry to hear that. And next week?"

"We'll have to see."

He set his briefcase on his Audi, which was parked next to the Porsche. "I am a very determined man, Mr. Foster. Assure your wife that neither I nor this issue are going to disappear into the woodwork just because she'd prefer it that way."

"At the moment, what my wife prefers or doesn't prefer regarding your so-far unsubstantiated claim is immaterial," Sterling said flatly. "Kate is in the hospital."

"I'm sorry to hear that." Ben shoved his free hand in his pocket, staring blindly at the well-appointed garage surrounding him. It had been built to his specifications, able to hold all three of his cars, the Harley that he never had time to ride anymore and his speedboat, with space to spare. It had meant excavating another two stories beneath the existing historic house he'd been determined to save, but he was a Robinson, which, at the time, had been the end of the story as far as he'd been concerned. But it was a reminder that all the wealth in the world couldn't prevent some things.

It hadn't convinced Stephanie six months ago to let Ben remain Henry's father—not once the toddler's real father proved his claim—and it wouldn't stop age from hitting them all. Even Kate Fortune, who'd looked so much younger than her ninety years.

"I hope it's not serious," he said truthfully, even though frustration bubbled inside him. "Is she here in Austin, or have you gone back to Minnesota?"

"Austin. She's not well enough to travel."

And that statement could mean just about anything, Ben figured. He didn't bother asking for details because he knew the other man wouldn't divulge them. Not until Kate believed the truth about Gerald, and maybe not even then. "I know you won't believe me, but if there is anything I can do, just ask. Give your wife my regards."

Finally, Sterling's voice showed some warmth. And a strong edge of irony. "Knowing my wife, I imagine she'll be in touch soon enough. Good night, Mr. Robinson," he said and ended the call.

But he remembered Ella still waiting on the other line. He thumbed his phone. "Still there?"

"Yes."

"That was Sterling Foster on my other line." Briefcase in hand, he entered the elevator that he'd installed more for the convenience of moving large pieces of furniture and the like than to save on steps.

"Kate Fortune's husband?"

He wasn't surprised that she knew that fact, even though it wasn't one they'd specifically discussed. She'd been at the same party; she'd heard Kate's speech, too. "Yes. She'd promised to meet my father this week, but she's in the hospital."

"Oh, dear. I hope she's all right."

"Yeah. If she never sees Gerald for herself, she's never going to acknowledge he's Jerome Fortune."

"Would that be the end of the world?" Her voice was soft. Tentative. "After all, it doesn't change the fact that he is. Nor does it change the fact that you and your brothers and sisters are Fortunes, too, regardless of the Robinson name. I mean, blood is blood. Isn't it?"

Talking to Ella had eased his irritation, but she had no way of knowing the bite her last comment contained. And it had nothing to do with the Fortune mess and everything to do with losing Henry. "That's what I hear."

He stepped off the elevator on the fourth floor that was completely occupied by his master suite. Nearly two walls of the floor were windows, and without turning on any lights he could see rivulets of rain running down them. "You wait until the car comes for you in the morning," he reminded her.

"If it's raining, I will." She waited a beat. "Ben? Are—are you all right?"

He looked at his wide bed, instantly imagining her vibrant hair spread across the steel-gray sheets, and closed his eyes.

But it didn't make it any better.

He opened his eyes and carried his briefcase to the sleek built-in rosewood dresser and set his briefcase on top, next to the only framed picture of Henry he had. He kept putting the damn thing in the trash, but Mrs. Stone kept retrieving it and setting it back on his dresser.

He turned the photo facedown.

"I'm fine." His tone was abrupt. He was her employer. Period. He could imagine anything he wanted about her, but that was as far as it would ever go. "Good night, Ella."

Chapter Five

The rain stopped long before morning.

Ella told herself she wasn't disappointed when she awakened to a dry, clear sky. It was so clear, in fact, that she decided to bicycle to work.

She also returned to her usual blue jeans and thermal shirt.

The tone in her boss's voice when he'd ended his strange call the night before had strongly reminded her that she was only an employee. And a temporary one, at that.

Her mom wouldn't get off shift for another few hours, and Ella saw Rory off to school as usual, then pulled on her bicycle helmet, crossed the strap of her messenger bag across her chest and set off on her bike. She was determined to enjoy the fresh, crisp air and the ride, and to focus on the exorbitantly generous financial incentive waiting for her at the end of this job she'd been hired to do.

When she was finished working for Ben, for the first time she'd be able to be a full-time student, to take a full load of classes instead of one or two at a time, and that would put her on track to graduate in only three semesters. Compared to the three or four *years* she'd been looking at otherwise, it was a definite motivator.

And she needed to stop thinking of her boss as *Ben*. He was Ben Robinson. Maybe if she used his whole name every time she thought of him, she wouldn't be so inclined to dream about him.

She didn't work for Ben. She worked for Ben Robinson.

"Ben Robinson," she said out loud as she stopped in front of a busy coffee shop near his house. Then she laughed at herself because she was sounding decidedly lunatic.

"Excuse me?"

She smiled at the waitress who was cleaning off a metal table set on the sidewalk. "Just talking to myself," she said and locked up her bike before going quickly inside.

She'd planned her schedule to arrive in plenty of time to avoid being "late" in Mrs. Stone's calculations, but only if she didn't waste too much of it standing in line. Ten minutes later, she set off again, covered coffee cup in hand. After that, it took no time at all to reach Ben's—*Ben Robinson's!*—house, where she locked up her bicycle again outside the front door, latching the chain around a narrow tree planted next to the street. She rang the bell and pulled off her helmet, and when Mrs. Stone hadn't answered after a second ring, she used the key and let herself in.

She was just heading up the first flight of stairs when Mrs. Stone appeared above her, carrying a feather duster. Of course the housekeeper immediately zeroed in on the coffee cup Ella was carrying. "If you wanted coffee, you should have said." Then she passed Ella on the steps, going down without another word.

Just another day in paradise, Ella thought, and continued up to Ben's—darn it, *Ben Robinson's*—office. He'd obviously looked over the notes she'd left for him, adding a few handwritten comments in the margin. He'd also left the names of three more women with whom his father had likely had affairs.

Three. It boggled the mind how one man—a married man, at that—could have had so many dalliances. *And* that his son knew about them.

She couldn't imagine what sort of marriage Gerald must have.

But then, she wasn't being paid by Ben Robinson—yes, that was better; it would just take practice—to conjecture about the legitimate Robinson family. Her task was merely to find the illegitimate.

Literally.

She left her messenger bag and helmet on the table next to the windows, then settled down at the computer, picking up where she'd left off the evening before. The task felt less like looking for a needle in the haystack than it had the previous day, and with each click of the mouse, she felt a growing excitement. When she opened a conference program saved on the website of a Boston-based software firm and saw the list of employees involved, the hairs on the back of her neck even prickled. Because there was Randy Phillips, complete with a small photograph and an accompanying bio extolling his Cornell University education and his early childhood growing up in Denver, Colorado.

If he wasn't Antonia Bell's son, she'd eat her hat.

The black-and-white photograph showed he possessed hair just as dark as her boss's and light-colored eyes that might very well be just as blue.

She'd been instructed to call Ben immediately when she had news, but there was no phone on the desk and she didn't possess a cell phone. She left the office, looking around the living area, and didn't see one there, either.

The man ran one of the largest computer firms in the world, but he didn't have a darned phone?

She stood in the middle of the spacious room, eyeing the two closed doors on the wall opposite the windows overlooking the river. "Mrs. Stone," she called out, but naturally, the woman couldn't choose that time to appear.

She went to the closest door and knocked before gingerly opening it. She expected a closet. Or maybe the kitchen. But she was instead greeted by a stunning bedroom that had an unused air about it.

She tried the second door and found a child's room, charmingly decorated in red and yellow trains. There were dozens of toys clearly meant for a young child on the bright blue shelves. A gloriously beautiful crib that looked straight out of a magazine was positioned in the center of the room beneath a mobile that seemed to hang magically out of clear space. There was not a speck of dust or a single item out of place.

Nevertheless, this room, too, felt unused. She remembered the photograph she'd found in Ben's desk the first day she'd started and felt inexplicably sad as she pulled the door closed again.

When she turned, Mrs. Stone was standing behind her, and Ella jumped.

"That room is off-limits."

"Then maybe it should be locked," Ella pointed out breathlessly, pressing her hand to her thumping chest. "I was looking for a phone!"

Mrs. Stone's lips pressed together. "The telephone is built into the Mister's computer," she said as if everyone should know that.

Ella felt herself flush. "Obviously, I didn't know that." She returned to the office and sat back at the desk. A few mouse clicks later, and she discovered the telephone app and dialed the number that Ben had left for her. It was answered immediately by a woman who told her that Ben was unavailable. Disappointed, Ella left her name and hung up.

With nothing else to do, she moved on to the next pro-
spective baby mama, and spent the rest of the day—save
the ten minutes she took to consume the wedge salad and
club sandwich Mrs. Stone delivered—pouring through
vital-statistic websites.

She rode her bicycle back home again at the end of
the day.

Ben hadn't called. Nor had he come home for lunch
again.

And even though the sky was still dry and still clear,
the day felt gloomy as a result.

Ben looked from his pile of messages to Bonita. "Why
didn't you tell me about this?" He held up the one from
Ella between two fingers.

Bonita eyed him, obviously unperturbed by his per-
turbation. "One or another of your women calls and begs
to speak to you on a daily basis. If you want me to bring
your attention to them each and every time, you'll never
get out of this office."

"Ella's not one of my women."

Bonita made a disbelieving face. "Then who is she?"

She'd worked for him since before he'd become COO.
There were no secrets he'd ever kept from her. Until now.
But he was damned if he could come up with a lie. "She's
a friend. *Just* a friend," he said with emphasis, trying to
forestall her smirk.

"Sure. Like you have female friends." Bonita left a
folder of correspondence on his desk. "Those need your
signatures tonight. They need to go out tomorrow."

He hated signing letters. "You could have signed them
for me. You sign my name better than I do."

"A good reason for me *not* to," she pointed out wryly,
and left his office. "Sign them. *Then* go out and play with
Ella the friend," she said loudly from her desk.

Wes walked in a moment later and tossed a thick binder in front of him. "Who's Ella?"

Ben looked pointedly at the opened door behind his brother and Wes pushed it closed.

"She's the person I hired to find out if Dad has other children out there."

Wes's lips thinned. Ben knew good and well that his twin didn't share his feelings on locating their father's illegitimate offspring. If there were any. "Like there aren't already enough Robinsons," he muttered. "If it's not that, it's your damn 'Fortune business.'" He air-quoted the term before gesturing at the binder. "Those are all the PRDS on the latest apps we're developing."

"I was expecting a page of bullet points, not full-on product requirement docs." Ben lifted the binder an inch and let it drop back on his desk with a thud. "Either give me a ten-second skinny that I can report back to Dad when I have dinner with him tonight, or come and do it yourself."

Wes's lips twisted even more. He retrieved the binder and opened the door. "Fine. Give me ten minutes."

Ben exhaled, wishing he knew what to do to ease the tension between his brother and himself. But he couldn't change being COO of Robinson Tech. Didn't want to change it. Nor was he willing to call off his hunt for Gerald's offspring or give up this "Fortune business."

"Bonita," he barked. "Go home and cook dinner on time for your husband for once."

She appeared in his doorway, one hand on her generous hip. "Have you signed those letters?"

He dutifully picked up his pen and flipped open the folder. "Satisfied?"

"Mildly."

He scrawled his name at the bottom of the first page and flipped to the second. "Go home," he repeated. "I'm not paying you overtime."

"How do you know? I *do* sign your name better than you do," she reminded him with a sly smile. "And I'll leave. With pleasure. But I won't cook for Enrique. He always cooks for *me*." Waggling her fingers in a wave, she disappeared from view again and a moment later, he heard her leave.

He dropped his pen on the desk and dialed Ella's number. This time, he didn't assume she'd be the one to answer, but she was.

"I didn't know you'd called until a few minutes ago," he said. "Did you find him? Our Randy Phillips?"

"Yes. I don't have his home address or anything, but he works for a small software firm in Boston named BRD Systems. Assuming their staff listing on their website is accurate, he's the senior programmer there."

"Excellent." His fingers tightened around the receiver.

"Do you want me to try to contact him or anything?"

"No. I'll take care of that."

"I also have a possible line on a woman in Chicago," she offered. "Do you want me to proceed with that, or…?"

"Absolutely." He wished to hell he hadn't scheduled a dinner meeting with his father. But he'd done it earlier that week with the intention of presenting Kate Fortune to him. Her hospitalization had changed that plan, but not the fact that the old man expected to meet with Ben. "And next time you call my office, Bonita will put you through."

"Okay. Was there anything else, then?"

He frowned, picking up something distant in her tone that he couldn't explain. "No."

"Have a, uh, a nice evening, then."

"You, too." He didn't hang up until the line went dead. He finished signing his letters, then headed out, barely remembering to stop by Wes's office for his bullet list because he was too preoccupied with Ella's call.

Even though the official dinner hour at the Robinson estate wasn't for another few hours, he drove out there now, feeling the same itchy tension he'd been feeling ever since his sister Rachel had reconnected with them after being away for several years.

He'd been glad she hadn't written off the entire family—when she'd up and moved away with no rhyme or reason that he'd understood at the time, he'd wondered—but the information she'd returned with about Gerald's true identity had sent him spinning. Even though their father denied it, that itch of Ben's had told him otherwise. It was an itch that still nagged, driving him to find what other secrets their father was harboring.

There were three other cars parked in the wide drive when he arrived; two belonged to his parents, and he didn't recognize the third. So that meant that Zoe, Olivia or Sophie were probably around, too. Ordinarily, he didn't mind running in to one of his little sisters, but Ben wanted to get in and out as quickly as possible so he could get on with the task of meeting Randy Phillips.

Because he *would* need to meet the guy.

He'd decided that the moment that Ella said she'd located him.

He went in the house through one of the rear doors, stopping to give his mother the obligatory kiss on her cheek when he spotted her sitting at the end of the table in the formal dining room. She had papers spread around her—probably some event or another from one of her charities—and she gave Ben as much attention as he gave her. Had she ever shown more warmth to the children she'd borne Gerald Robinson, it might have been different.

But Ben had gotten more affection from the cook than he ever had his own mother.

"Dad?"

"His office, of course," Charlotte said, barely lifting her platinum-blond head.

He left her to her paperwork and strode through the house. When he found his father in his office, Gerald was pacing in front of the windows, his cell phone at his ear. Ben was waved in and he took one of the leather chairs in front of the desk, drumming his thumb silently on the arm until his father completed his call and eyed him, arching one of his dark, prominent brows.

"Thought you were coming later for dinner."

"I thought I was, too, but something's come up that I need to take care of."

Gerald gave him an inquiring look, but Ben wasn't biting. Instead, he gave his father the thumbnail sketch of everything he'd been overseeing for the past two weeks, beginning with the Japan acquisition and ending with Wes's information on the latest products under development and the status of the dating app they were gearing up to launch soon. He kept the conversation strictly on company business. The last time he'd veered off that, they'd gotten into a shouting match about Gerald's past that Ben had no interest in repeating. As a result, he got out of the meeting with his dad in just under thirty minutes.

He was back in his own home office less than half an hour after that, where he pored over the information that Ella had left him. Armed with the name of Randy's employer, Ben did some of his own research and discovered that the vice president of BRD System was a fellow Wharton alum.

He smiled.

The phone rang, jerking Ella awake.

She'd dozed off over her Intro to Taxation textbook.

She swiped her hand over her bleary face and got up

from the table, where she'd been reading-slash-dozing, and grabbed the phone before it could ring again. "'Lo?"

"Ella?"

She went wide-awake as a shiver danced down her spine from the sound of Ben's deep voice. *That's supposed to be Ben Robinson, remember?*

She ignored the acerbic voice of her conscience. "Hi, Ben." Just saying his name made something inside her chest feel soft. A glance at her watch told her it was nearly ten and she sank down on the arm of the couch. "What's up?"

"We're going to Boston in the morning."

She blinked. His voice had been distinctly edgy. "I'm sorry?"

"Pack for overnight."

"You…ah…you want me to go *with* you to Boston?"

"I just said that. Weather is a lot colder, too. They just got dumped with about a foot of snow, so bring a winter coat if you've got one."

Her common sense tried to pour water over the excitement sparking inside her belly. "I can't just go off to Boston."

"Why not?"

"Because I—" She looked down the hall, and could hear her brother's video game through the closed door. "Can I call you back in a few minutes?"

"We'll have separate hotel rooms, Ella, if that's what's worrying you."

Her stomach hollowed out at the mere thought of *not* having separate rooms. "It wasn't. I'll call you right back." Before he could say whether he liked it or not, she pressed a shaking finger against the Disconnect button. Then she got to her feet and paced in front of the couch while she dialed her mother's number at work.

"What's wrong?" Elaine immediately asked. "Is Rory—"

"He's fine," she assured her quickly. "I'm sorry to bother you at work, but, um, but my boss wants me to go with him to Boston tomorrow, and—"

"Boston!" Elaine sounded as surprised as Ella still felt.

"—and I couldn't agree without talking to you first. You're still on nights, and Rory would be alone."

"Is this business or pleasure?"

"Mom!" Ella felt her face flush and was glad her mother couldn't see it. "Business, of course. But we'd be staying overnight. Rory would be alone."

"Honey…" Elaine's voice softened. "Worrying about your brother is my job, not yours. Of course you'll go to Boston. When else would you ever have an opportunity like this?"

"Are you sure?"

"You are more of a worrywart than I am," her mother chided gently. "I'm sure. And if I weren't sure, I'd tell you to go, anyway. I can take a day of vacation if I need to. But I'll work that out with Rory. He's almost seventeen. He's naturally going to think he's old enough to stay by himself for a night."

"He says I'll need a winter coat."

Fortunately, her mother interpreted the "he" to mean her boss, rather than her brother. "I have a wool peacoat," she said. "It's old, but they never go out of style. You can use that. You'll be fine, Ella. Now, before you argue with me for another ten minutes, I'm going to hang up. I love you."

Ella's "Love you, too," was said to a dial tone.

She pressed her palm to her jumpy stomach and redialed Ben's number. "I can go."

"What were you doing? Checking with your boyfriend?"

Her palm was sweaty against the phone and she switched hands. "Of course not."

"He doesn't care if you go off to Boston with a man?"

Her stomach swooped. "I'm not going off to Boston with a man. I'm accompanying my boss on a business trip. And even if there *was* a boyfriend, that's not something I'd have to ask permission to do! If you must know, I was letting my mother know because she works nights. Which means my sixteen-year-old brother will be left alone tomorrow night. And that's not something we usually do. Satisfied?" She felt breathless.

"Quite." He waited a beat. "You can let your mother know you'll be at the Boston Harbor Hotel. I'll send a car to pick you up in the morning. Can you be ready by seven?"

"Yes. I assume this means you want to check out Randy Phillips in person?"

"I spoke with him already."

Shock had her sitting again on the arm of the couch. As paranoid as he'd been about keeping his hunt on the down-low, she couldn't believe Ben would have told Randy his suspicion that they were half brothers. "I guess you found his personal contact information," she said faintly.

"I told him he'd come to the attention of Robinson Tech and we'd like to talk to him about a job. He thought I was a recruiter. You'll take the meeting with him."

Horror accosted her. "Me!"

"At the risk of sounding conceited, he'd probably recognize me. You're quick on your feet. You can act the part of an HR rep. It'll be easier than pretending to be a bartender."

"Thanks, I think."

"I'll see you at the airport, then. G'night, Ella."

"Good night." But once again, she found herself speaking to a dial tone.

She replaced the receiver.

Her dull textbook was lying open on the dining room table, her highlighting pen uncapped beside it, drying out.

Rory's video game was still blaring from behind his bedroom door.

Everything was normal around her.

But inside, she felt anything but normal.

She was going to Boston.

With Ben.

Chapter Six

He'd neglected to warn her that he wasn't just sending any old car to pick her up.

It was a limousine.

Long.

Black.

And noticeable to everyone in the neighborhood who was up and about when it pulled to a stop in front of the small Thomas home the next morning at 6:58 a.m.

Bernie even left his front porch to walk to the shrubs that separated their yards to get a closer look. "Going somewhere, Ella?"

She handed over the satchel she was using as a suitcase to the black-suited young man who'd come to the door for her and waved at Bernie. "Boston," she said. "I'll be back tomorrow. Mom's still on nights, so keep an ear out for Rory, will you?"

The old man nodded with a wave. "Maybe I'll let 'im beat me at chess."

Ella smiled, holding back her laughter, because everyone on their block knew about Rory's chess prowess. "I'm sure he'd like that," she called back.

The driver had placed her canvas bag in the trunk of the car and was waiting by the opened rear door.

She nervously tugged on the end of her ponytail. "I'll just be another second," she told him, and darted back inside.

Rory was still sitting at the table eating his breakfast cereal. She gave him a kiss on his cheek that he made a face over. "I'm not a baby," he grumbled. "Just go on, wouldja?"

"Don't be late for your bus," she instructed one last time before she grabbed the peacoat she'd unearthed from the hall closet and hurried out the door again, closing it behind her.

Aware of the driver watching her impassively, she modified her instinctive dash down the cracked driveway to a more dignified walk, tugging at the hem of her navy blue blazer as she went. The driver took the coat from her arm before she climbed in the backseat, then handed it back to her before closing her, literally, in the lap of luxury.

She sank back into the buttery leather seat, staring at the plush interior. There was a small television screen built in to the center console between the two thickly padded fold-down seats directly opposite the seat she occupied. It was switched on to a news network, though the sound was off. The console between her enveloping seat and the one next to her provided not only the expected armrest, but also a panel of buttons that presumably operated the television and who knew what else. A drawer below that offered gleaming crystal glasses and two full-sized bottles of wine.

Bemused, she pushed the drawer closed and stared out the window beside her. The ride was so smooth it was undetectable, and with the interior as soundproof as it was, she had to look out the window to be certain they were even moving. And it took her a moment longer before she realized they weren't heading to the airport.

There was no way for her to see the driver from where she sat. The area that might have held a partition looked instead like thickly padded leather upholstery behind the fold-down seats. She studied the panel of buttons next to her and pushed a control marked with a faint IC that she hoped stood for *intercom*. "Hello?"

A disembodied voice responded. "Yes, ma'am."

Success. "Are we picking up Mr. Robinson after all?"

"No, ma'am."

She studied the freeway. "Aren't we supposed to meet him at the airport?"

"An executive field, ma'am, where your charter is waiting. Not Austin-Bergstrom. We're only five minutes out now."

"Thank you."

"My pleasure, ma'am."

She released the button. She'd only flown a few times in her life and always on a commercial jet. Now, she had images of tiny little planes hovering in her brain and she wasn't sure how she felt about that at all.

The five minutes passed all too quickly and the car smoothly stopped beneath a high, arching canopy in front of a long, modern-looking structure of glass and steel. The driver walked around the vehicle and retrieved her satchel from the trunk, then opened the door for her. "Mr. Robinson will meet you in the lobby through there." He gestured at the building where it curved in a half circle of windows that overlooked the stretch of manicured grass following the road.

She draped her coat over her arm and took the satchel from him. "Thank you." If she hesitated, the butterflies inside her would turn into raging dragons, so she walked quickly through the doorway that slid open at her approach.

There was nothing about the interior of the building that reminded her of an airport. No ticket counters. No security gates. Just a few dozen leather chairs arranged in clusters, either directed to look out the windows, at the seriously ginormous television screen affixed high on a pale stone wall or at what was obviously a cocktail bar.

She'd no more taken a few steps, though, when Ben strode into view, his head down as he studied the phone in his long-fingered hand.

Before he noticed her, she inhaled shakily, her fingers tightening around the handle of her tote. He was wearing a pale gray suit with a perfectly knotted silver tie. His hair looked damp, slicked back from his face, only enhancing his sharply defined features.

He was…perfect.

And no amount of calling him "Ben Robinson" in her head seemed capable of stopping her heart from jumping in her chest when he glanced up from his phone and his piercing blue gaze pinned her in place.

Her mouth was dry and she swallowed, managing to find a smile from somewhere when he gave her an absent-looking one, before stopping a few feet away. He slid his phone into his lapel pocket and reached out his hand.

Fortunately, she realized he was merely reaching for her satchel before she did something really stupid, like place her sweaty palm into his.

He pulled the strap of her bag over his shoulder, not seeming to care that it looked like a poor relative to the deep brown leather garment bag already hanging there and the black coat slung carelessly over his other arm. "Every-thing okay with the car I sent?"

She nodded. "How could it not be?"

His lips twitched and he gestured toward the bar. "We still have a few minutes if you want something."

Dutch courage before seven-thirty in the morning? She gave the bar a skeptical look. "Do they have coffee?"

"Sure." He waited for her to precede him to the bar. As soon as they approached, a smiling girl appeared through a door, greeting him by name.

"Couple coffees to go, Marie."

"Sure thing." The attendant gave Ella a noticeably curious once-over as she worked. "Where are you headed to today?"

"Boston."

Marie gave an exaggerated shiver. "Cold." She set two tall cups on the gleaming granite bar and looked at Ella again. "Cream or sugar?"

"Neither, thank you."

Marie popped two covers on the cups and passed them to Ben. "Stay warm."

"No worries on that score." Ben handed one of the cups to Ella.

Marie's eyes went meaningfully from Ben to Ella. "I bet," she said with a knowing laugh, and turned to go back through the door again.

Ella couldn't help but wonder how many times Ben had flown off somewhere exotic from this airport with a woman on his arm with whom he *would* be sharing a hotel room.

"What about paying for the coffee?"

"Marie'll add it to my account." He seemed amused that she'd asked. "The gate's this way," he said, leading the way around the bar, down a gleaming tiled hallway to another area similar to the one in the front. Only here, the windows overlooked the airstrip and a half-dozen parked airplanes.

They didn't exactly look like the two-seater propeller jobs she'd envisioned, either. Instead they were all sleek-looking jets. The smallest one had eight porthole windows marching down the side.

"I don't think we're in Kansas anymore," she murmured.

Ben's smile crooked. He tucked his free hand around her elbow and she swallowed hard as he guided her toward a doorway that led out to the planes.

"No security lines to get through, I guess," she observed as they walked toward a white plane with no logos or lettering on it except for the series of numbers near the tail and the black stripe that ran the length of the body below the ten windows.

"Not yet."

The chilly breeze tugged at his tie the same way it did her ponytail. She looked away from the close fit of his white shirt against his abdomen before starting up the steps into the plane. She didn't have to duck to go through the doorway, though she noticed Ben—with a good ten or more inches on her own five-four—dipped his head a little.

Despite the number of windows on the plane, there were only four seats inside the spacious interior. Four large, incredibly comfortable-looking seats upholstered in cream-colored leather. Like the seats in the limousine, these also faced each other.

"Sit where you want."

She immediately took one facing the front of the plane and the doorway. She fit her coffee into one of the molded holders built into the side of the plane next to the seat.

"Don't want to fly facing backward?"

"Probably silly, but no. I don't."

He chuckled and opened an elaborate wood cabinet that was built into one side of the plane. He stored their bags inside, then their coats, before taking the seat across the "aisle" next to her, storing his coffee cup the same way she had. "Truth be told, I feel weird when I sit in those rear-facing seats, too. Like there's less control because I'm looking toward the tail of the plane. Crazy, because unless I'm in the cockpit, I don't have any control over the plane, anyway."

"Do you know how to fly a plane?"

"I got my private pilot's license years ago. Don't have time to do it very often anymore. Not with my responsibilities at Robinson Tech."

The cockpit door ahead of them looked like it was made out of the same shining wood as the cabinet. It opened to reveal a uniformed man with salt-and-pepper hair, who told them they would be getting underway in only a few minutes.

"Thanks, Michael." Ben waited for the door to close again before looking at Ella. "He's the captain. If you saw through the door, you probably noticed Veronica, too. She's the copilot."

"Do they work for Robinson Tech?"

He shook his head, pulling his seat belt across his lean hips. "No, but I use them a lot. You got your belt fastened okay?"

She pushed the buckle together and they both heard the click. "I'm good."

"We should be there by noon. Phillips is meeting us—" he shot her a quick look "—*you*, at one o'clock for lunch at one of the hotel restaurants. But if you're hungry before then—" he gestured at the large cabinet holding their luggage "—there is plenty of food and such here on the plane. You can't see them, but there's a fridge and a microwave inside there, too."

She grinned because she never would have imagined Ben Robinson playing flight attendant. "No espresso machine?"

One corner of his lips lifted. "Oh, yeah. There's one of those, too." He lifted his coffee cup out of the holder and held it up. "So if you're caffeine-addicted like me, you'll be in good shape."

It was too easy becoming sidetracked by the half smile on his face instead of thinking like she should about the reason she was on this plane with him in the first place. "I hope I don't blow things for you when I meet with Randy. I'm not sure it's such a good idea for me to pretend to be someone actually from Robinson Tech. I'm not much of an actress."

"You'll be fine. Ask him about his education. His career goals."

"How does that get you any closer to knowing if he's your half brother?"

He gave her a sidelong look. "Trust me. Most guys are ready and willing to talk to a pretty girl like you about just about anything."

Warmth rose through her and she was glad the engines suddenly revved and the plane began moving smoothly away from the building and the other planes.

"And then what?" she asked above the engines. "Do you know what you're going to do if you decide he *is* your half brother? Are you just going to tell him what you suspect? Do you want a blood test or anything to prove—"

"Blood tests aren't definitive," he said abruptly. He took a drink from his coffee cup before replacing it in the holder. "Not unless they're ruling out paternity."

"Then a DNA test," she ventured. "Will you want one of those?"

He didn't look her way, but she still saw the way his lips twisted. "It'd be the smart thing to do."

"You don't seem very happy about that," she offered tentatively. "Are you sure you want to proceed with this interview charade at all?"

He exhaled. When he looked at her again, his expression was smooth once more. "I'm sure."

The plane had reached the runway and it stopped moving while the engines ran even faster. Ella reflexively cupped her fingers more tightly around the armrests.

"Are you a nervous flyer?"

She shot him a glance. "Considering my wealth of experience from the two times I've ever flown? Who can say?"

"You've only flown twice before?"

"School trips when I was in high school. Seattle my junior year and San Francisco when I was a senior."

"So you've never been to Boston."

She shook her head. "Nope."

"Well, then." His eyes crinkled slightly. "It would be unpatriotic of me if we didn't fit in a little sightseeing."

"Unpatriotic?"

"Location of the Boston Tea Party? Walking the Freedom Trail?"

"Sure. With a foot of snow on the ground."

"Tourism doesn't stop just from a little snow. Any self-respecting Bostonian would probably tell you that."

"How am I going to have time to sightsee? We're coming back home tomorrow."

He gave her a dry look. "The point of a charter, Ella, is that it flies according to my convenience."

She couldn't help the laugh that burst out of her. "Do you have any idea how spoiled you sound?"

His lips twitched. "Not spoiled. Simply accustomed to getting what I pay for."

She didn't even realize the plane had begun speeding down the runway until the momentum pressed her back in her seat when the wheels left the ground. "And I'm here to tell you, Mr. Robinson, that most people don't go around chartering planes! At least not in my experience."

He smiled widely enough to reveal the flash of an entirely unexpected dimple. "All twenty-three years of it, hmm?"

She huffed and crossed her arms, looking away. But she knew the effect was ruined because she couldn't seem to get the stupid smile off her face. The man wasn't making it any easier for her to put her silly crush on him to bed once and for all when he was being so, well, so *likable*. "As if you're so ancient," she drawled. "Thirty-three? Please."

"Who told you how old I am?"

"The magazine article I told you about," she said as if the answer was obvious. When in fact she had no idea whatsoever if the article had included any such personal details. No, she had the internet to thank for that particular fact, but she didn't particularly want to advertise her cybersnooping. It was too embarrassing. Too…revealing. As if he'd interpret her interest as more than professional. And it was, but still. "I suppose you've traveled all over."

His eyes were laughing. "A few places."

She named the most exotic place that popped into her head. "Istanbul?"

He nodded once. "Yes, I've been to Turkey. Israel. Egypt, Kenya, Madagascar. South Africa. Pretty much all of northern Europe." His eyes narrowed in thought. "Not Finland. Don't remember being in Finland."

"Oh." She waved her hand. "Well, then, clearly you haven't *really* traveled."

He laughed softly, and the sound of it seemed to make something inside her chest swell. To cover, she took a long sip from her coffee cup.

The plane had leveled out and the sound of the engines had softened to a low, steady hum that was barely discernible. "What's your favorite place?"

"Austin, Texas, US of A," he said immediately.

"I'm surprised. But that's certainly spoken like a Texan."

"If the boot fits."

She gave his well-shined shoes a pointed look. "Have you ever even worn boots?"

"Can you be a Texan without having done so?"

"Perhaps not," she said humorously. "Your boots are probably custom-made with hand-tooled leather and God knows what else."

"I believe they were custom Castletons."

"Castleton boots aren't in most people's budgets even when they're *not* custom."

"I can't help that. How many pairs of boots do you have?"

She shrugged. "Two. One for dress. One for casual. And they're certainly not Castletons, but I've had them forever, too. Ever since high school."

He coughed slightly, but not quickly enough to mask the laugh that it really was. "So *really* old," he said after he'd recovered.

Because it did sound a bit ridiculous, she smiled, too. Well, that and the fact that it was fairly impossible not to smile when Ben Robinson was looking at you that way. "I have more boots than I have suits," she drawled, tugging at her blazer. "And more textbooks than both. I brought my taxation book and it's taking up as much space in my bag as my clothes."

"Textbooks. I remember the day. Do you really have physical books anymore or ebooks?"

"A mix." She didn't really want to get on the topic of digital books because it might lead to talk of computers and other magical electronic devices, which would lead to having her brother's avid interest in all things Robinson Tech bouncing around inside her head. "Depends on the class," she explained, which held enough truth not to make her skin heat. She took a sip of her coffee and made a point of looking out the window beside her.

The plane was slicing through bands of wispy white

clouds that still allowed her to see the checkerboard landscape far below. "It's so pretty," she murmured.

"Things are always prettier from a distance."

She looked back at him. "I don't know if that's very profound, or if it's very sad."

"Closer you get, the more you see the flaws. The devil's always in the details."

"No computer would exist today if it weren't for those devilish details. Can't imagine you could have any computer system that—" she waved her hand in the space between their seats "—glosses over anything. One missed circuit, one missed connection, one missed wire or screw or filament or programming logic?" She shrugged. "Then you've got a hunk of useless hardware sitting around collecting dust, don't you? Computers in our phones. Computers in our cars. Computers as small as my thumbnail and as large as entire warehouses. This plane is probably run as much by a computer as Captain Michael up there."

She shook her head and looked out the window again at the checkerboard squares below. "If it weren't for some farmer—goodness knows how many farmers and workers are down there plowing fields, planting some, resting others—I wouldn't be able to look at it from a distance and appreciate how pretty it is." She glanced at him again. "Devil's not in those details any more than the devil's in... what do they call them? The facilities where you make computer chips and stuff?"

"You mean clean rooms?"

She nodded. "I don't need distance to see the prettiness. I'll take the details."

"Spoken like a future accountant."

She smiled. "And if everything works out with this job you hired me for, I'll be able to call myself one long before I thought I would."

"You've already made enough progress to take us to

Boston." His voice was calm and certain. "Of course everything will work out."

She inhaled a quick breath and forced a suddenly shaky smile.

Of course everything would work out. How could it not?

Chapter Seven

When they landed in Boston, the sky was solid, leaden.

Ben watched Ella wrap herself in the ancient-looking coat and turn up the collar against the stiff, cold breeze that sliced over them even in the short distance from the terminal to the familiar black Town Car waiting for them.

She ducked her head and quickly climbed into the rear of the car ahead of him. And even though Ben had never felt the space inside the vehicle was confining, it did when he sat down beside her.

And even though he felt warm in the heated car—overly so, thanks to her closeness—it was obvious that she didn't, considering the way she balled her hands up inside the bottoms of her coat sleeves after fastening her seat belt. "You need a scarf and gloves."

She immediately poked her hands back out, as if she'd been caught doing something wrong. "I have mittens inside my bag." And it was being stowed as she spoke in the trunk by their gray-haired driver, Johnny, who climbed behind the wheel a moment later.

"Your water taxi will be waiting, Mr. Robinson," Johnny said as he worked his way out into the stream of taxis and buses continually pulling up and pulling out from the airport terminal.

Ben's attention was on Ella's face. Her pert nose was red from the cold.

"I think you'd better cancel the water taxi and just drive us into the city."

"Oh, but—" Ella looked dismayed. "Isn't the hotel right across the harbor?"

"Pretty much."

"The water taxi has a heated cabin," Johnny reminded, "but I'm at your disposal for your entire stay here in Boston the same as always. If you want me to drive you around—"

"Yes," Ben instructed. He had to steel himself against her palpable disappointment. He pulled out his cell phone and blindly scrolled through one message after another. "We'll still get you on the water, Ella. Promise."

Ella felt rather like a schoolgirl who'd just been told she'd still get her treat. And even though she'd looked forward to the novel experience of a water taxi—supposedly one of the easiest ways to travel from the airport—she wasn't here for pleasure. She twisted her watch around so she could see her watch face. "We're meeting Randy in less than thirty minutes."

"You're meeting him." He slid his phone in his pocket again and gave her a distracted look. "We've got enough time," he assured her. "And even if we were late, he'd wait."

Because Randy thought he was being interviewed for a legitimate position with Robinson Tech.

She knew how intently Ben was looking forward to

learning more about the other man, but she still couldn't help feeling as though she was part of a great deception.

And the closer they came to her supposed "interview" with Randy Phillips, the tighter the knots got in her stomach.

The drive from the airport to their hotel took less time than she'd expected and before she was at all prepared, she was hurrying to keep up with Ben as he strode through the lobby with the attractive, long-legged hotel representative who personally showed them to their rooms.

The moment Ella stepped across the threshold of her room, she was entranced by the view out the window opposite her. She was vaguely aware of the bellman depositing her satchel on a rack as if it was just as fine a piece of luggage as Ben's, but she couldn't help walking straight to the picture window overlooking the harbor and peering out even if it did make her look like a kid with her first view of Santa Claus.

Despite the sky that had turned gray before they'd landed, the view was simply spectacular. And she knew it couldn't have come inexpensively.

She looked over her shoulder at the king-size bed, the wing chairs and gleaming desk. Half of the house in which she lived could have fit into the spacious room.

Then she realized Ben was standing in the doorway looking amused, along with Long Legs and the bellman—both of whom wore kind, discreet smiles.

"Think it'll do?"

She refrained from falling back on the sumptuous-looking bed and gave him a look. "Are you sure this isn't supposed to be *your* room?"

"Mr. Robinson is in one of our suites," Long Legs said. She crossed the room and wrote on a small notepad sitting next to a complicated-looking telephone. "I'm writing his room number down for you," she said, "as well as my personal number. Should you need anything at all, please don't hesitate to reach out to me, day or night." She set down the pen just so next to the pad and returned to the doorway. "Would you like Jeremy here to show you the features of the room?"

Jeremy was too similar to Jerome, which served to remind her of her purpose there. "I'm fine." She unbuttoned her coat and focused on Ben. He was clearly a familiar face here at the hotel, but Ella couldn't imagine that he would have filled them in on the actual nature of his business there. Not this time. "I'll just freshen up and head down for the meeting. I'll report in afterward."

Ben nodded and the three of them left, pulling the door closed after them.

Alone in the elegant room, Ella's shoulders fell and she dragged off the coat, tossing it on one of the lovely coral-colored wing chairs. She brushed her hands down the sides of her navy blue blazer and opened her satchel to retrieve the zippered cosmetic case. Then she went into the bathroom, catching her breath all over again amid the gleam of crystal and marble.

Her eyes in the mirror looked as shell-shocked as she felt, and it probably wasn't a look that belonged on a representative from Robinson Tech.

She swiped some blush over her cheeks to brighten them up, and pulled her hair free from the ponytail. She worked her hairbrush through the long strands, not sure if she looked better or worse with her hair down. Ultimately, she decided to weave it away from her face in a loose braid that seemed a little more sophisticated then her usual ponytail. Her expression was still on the verge of making her seem like a wide-eyed bumpkin, but there was nothing she could do about that and she turned her back on her reflection, marching smartly back into the bedroom. Not letting herself become distracted by the view again, she pulled out a portfolio that held her notepad and a pen. She didn't have a briefcase, but at least the leather-looking portfolio cover seemed somewhat professional. She tucked it beneath her arm, slid her room key into her blazer pocket and, without stopping to let the sheer nervousness inside her go from bubbling to boiling over, left the room.

There was a couple already in the elevator when it stopped at Ella's floor. They were arm in arm and seemed oblivious to Ella's presence, considering the way they were locked on one another. In fact, Ella stood right in front of the doors, keeping her eyes trained on the floor display just to keep from feeling like a voyeur.

Mercifully, the elevator speedily dropped without stopping at any floors other than the lobby, and she quickly bolted from the car as soon as the doors parted. She made her way to the restaurant where she was to meet Randy. As soon as she gave her name, the hostess showed her to a table next to the window looking out on the wharf.

And a dark-haired man was already sitting there, looking out that window.

For a startled moment, adrenaline pumped through her. But then the man shifted in his seat, giving her a view of his profile, and she relaxed again.

She approached the table, her hand outstretched. "Mr. Phillips?"

His smile was wide. "Ms. Thomas." He stood and clasped her hand in a quick handshake.

"I'm sorry I'm late."

"Not at all." He gestured at the chair across from his. "I was early, actually." His smile was engaging. And while his eyes were light, as she'd seen from the online photo of him she'd found, they weren't blue at all, but a pale, amber brown. "Anxious, I guess," he admitted ruefully. "I'm still finding it a little surreal that Robinson Tech sought me out."

Conscience nipping, Ella somehow managed to keep her smile in place as she sat down and placed her notepad on the table. "Robinson Tech prides itself on employing the best and the brightest." She was merely quoting some of the tidbits she'd found on the Robinson Tech website, but it made Randy smile harder than ever.

A waiter approached then, giving Ella a reprieve before she had to begin the false interview. She ordered a glass of iced tea and a crab salad, which Randy dittoed, and all too quickly, the reprieve was over.

She folded her hands on top of her notepad. "So, Mr. Phillips—"

"Randy."

She smiled. "Why don't you tell me a little about yourself? What made you decide to go into programming?"

He sat forward a little, launching enthusiastically into what was obviously a well-prepared spiel.

She understood only a portion of the technical jargon he used, but figured that didn't really matter. She was supposedly a human resources representative. That didn't mean that she had to understand the finer points of everything he said. He was still talking when their meals arrived, and he broke off with a good-natured laugh as he sat back. "I could talk for hours, obviously."

She picked up her fork, "It's good to be passionate about your work."

"My parents were the same way."

Her grip tightened and she raised her eyebrows casually. "Oh?"

"Even before them, my grandparents were the same. My maternal grandmother started out in the tech industry back when most women—if they worked at all—were expected to be nurses and teachers. My mom followed in her footsteps."

She prodded a chunk of lettuce. "And your father?"

"Systems analyst. Retired a few years ago. How about you? Do you like working for Robinson Tech? Have you been with them long?"

She shoved a forkful of flaky, sweet crab in her mouth and gave a shrug and a nod that she hoped could mean most anything. "It's a dynamic company," she finally said.

A man in jogging gear trotted past the window, drawing the attention of both of them. "Did you grow up here in Boston?"

He shook his head. "Colorado, actually. My old man worked at the US Air Force Academy. That's where my parents met. We moved to Massachusetts when I was a teenager." He looked at her over their twin salads. "What about you? Robinson Tech is headquartered in Texas. Judging by the very attractive drawl you have, I'm guessing you've lived in Texas a while."

She smiled. "You might say that. Born and raised in Austin."

"Where y'all like to keep it weird, I hear."

She chuckled. "'Keep Austin Weird' has been a slogan there almost as long as I can remember." She lifted her shoulder. "We pride ourselves on being unique. Austin, Texas, is Austin, Texas. Not a carbon copy of any other city in Texas or elsewhere."

He grinned. "That's the word my mother uses to describe Austin. Unique. She lived there for a while before I was born. Actually worked for Robinson Tech for a brief time. It was Robinson Computers then, of course. Earlier days before the company really exploded into a global phenomenon." He leaned closer across the table, his voice dropping conspiratorially. "Her mother—my grandmother—told me once that she even had an affair with the man who founded the company."

Ella's fork slipped out of her suddenly lax fingers.

Randy chuckled and sat back. "Mom's never spoken

about it, so it's probably not true, anyway. But it makes for a good story." He gestured toward her, humor lighting his eyes. "Particularly with Robinson Tech now approaching me with the possibility of working there. Just goes to prove that the entire world is pretty darn weird, not just Austin, Texas."

Ella dabbed her napkin against her lips, gathering her composure. "I'm guessing all this happened before your mother married your dad," she finally managed to say with an immodestly impressive measure of drollness.

Randy's smile widened. "You'd think. But with my mom? Some things are hard to tell."

Ella laughed lightly. "Well, that sounds like a very interesting story." She deliberately met his eyes for a brief second, then looked away. But her effort of flirtation was ruined when her elbow knocked her notepad off the table. "Call me a klutz," she said wryly and leaned over to get it.

"You're too charming to be that," he assured, leaning over also.

Sitting across the room at the bar, Ben's hand tightened around the beer he'd been nursing for the past thirty minutes.

He knew he should have stayed up in his hotel suite.

But pacing around up there while wondering how Ella's meeting with Phillips was progressing had tested the always short limits of his patience. Yet being cooped up in his suite would have been preferable to watching Ella sit with the other man at that small window-side table as they laughed and smiled at each other.

"Would you like to see a menu, sir?"

He dragged his attention away from Ella and gave the bartender an impatient shake of his head. "I'll let you know if I do."

"Very good, sir." The bartender—a balding guy twice Ben's age—tilted his head in acknowledgment and moved away.

Ben knew he'd been short with the guy, but figured a fat tip would compensate. He looked back at Ella's table, only to see both her and Phillips bending down to the floor to pick up the thin brown book that had been sitting on the table beside Ella.

Ella's hand and Phillips's hand reached the thing at the same time, and the sight of her auburn head so close to Phillips's dark brown one sent something cold shooting through Ben's chest.

When he heard Ella's husky laugh and saw Phillips's appreciative smile, he set his icy pilsner glass on the bar with a thud and strode across to their table.

Before Ella had more than a second to notice his presence, he smiled into her face. "Surprise, sweetheart," he greeted her, and leaned down to kiss her smooth, soft cheek.

Her eyes went round, but to her credit, she didn't yank away from him too quickly. "Wh-what are you doing here?"

"Surprising you," he responded smoothly. He shot her companion a man-to-man look. "I ended up with some free time and wanted to surprise my fiancée. Looks like I succeeded."

Phillips looked almost as slack jawed as Ella as he popped out of his chair so fast he nearly tipped it over. "Mr. Robinson." He stuck out his hand. "It's an honor."

Ben shook the guy's hand. Briefly. And with a lot harder grip than necessary. "Mind if I steal Ella for a few minutes?" His words were a question but his tone was not, and Phillips would have had to have been an idiot not to realize it. "Then you can get on with your business."

"Of course I don't mind. I had no idea you two were engaged."

"It's recent." Ben wrapped his hand around Ella's, tugging lightly. "She swept me off my feet so fast, we haven't even had a chance to pick out her ring. Have we, honey?"

"It's been fast all right," she said, sounding a little choked. But she didn't pull her hand away from his and she set her napkin beside her plate and stood. "I'll be right back, Randy."

"Sure. Take your time."

Ben didn't wait to see Randy Phillips sit again. He tugged Ella after him right out of the restaurant. Only then did he release her hand.

Or rather, only then did she yank her hand away from his, like touching him was akin to touching a hot stove.

"*What* are you doing?" She kept her voice low, giving the few people milling around outside the restaurant entrance a wary look. "If you didn't trust me to handle the meeting, you could have just said so from the beginning and saved the effort of bringing me to Boston with you."

"It's not you I didn't trust. It's him."

She blinked. "Why?"

"You're a smart girl. Figure it out. The guy was obviously coming on to you."

"So what if he was? Don't you think that's to your advantage if he likes me a little? He was already talking about his personal life without me even having to prompt him." She propped her hands on her slender hips, which were closely outlined by the narrow blue suit she wore. "Now he thinks I'm engaged to the boss!" She practically hissed the term.

"He's here on a job interview."

"A fake one."

"He doesn't know that. And he's flirting with you. What kind of man does that during a business meeting?"

She snorted softly. "Most men, in my experience." Her soft words dripped sarcasm. "I'm not a complete babe in the woods, you know. I have had guys flirt with me before. I was handling Randy just fine until you swooped in and ruined it."

His jaw tightened. "I don't care if he's my half brother or not. He was leering at you."

She gaped. "He most certainly was not *leering*. We *were* two adults getting to know each other a little over a delightful lunch. What on earth did you expect? That I'd somehow ferret out his personal background and the identity of his birth father while pretending to review his professional résumé?"

Ben was used to controlling the situation. And he unquestionably was not controlling this one. "You're here at my request. Which makes your safety my responsibility."

She looked even more astounded. "Randy designs computer software. And if his excitement about doing so is any indication, he could even be an excellent addition to your company for real. How does that put my safety in question when we're in full view of at least fifty other people?"

"He was flirting," Ben said softly through his teeth.

Her cheeks flushed, making her eyes seem an even brighter shade of blue. "You flirted with me the first time we met," she reminded him. "I survived that just fine, too!"

Her boldness surprised the hell out of him. "I didn't flirt with you."

She pressed her lips together, giving him an incredulous look. "Firsts are always memorable," she finally said. "You said that to me that night at Kate Fortune's birthday party. Maybe you don't remember it. You probably don't remember it, because you're…well, you…and I'm just me. But you did, and at the time we both knew it was a *very* loaded comment. For someone *not* flirting."

He was never going to win this particular debate.

Primarily because Ella was right.

He had flirted with her that night. He remembered every single moment of that evening, just one short week ago.

And he did not like seeing Randy Phillips flirt with her now.

Or maybe he didn't like seeing her flirt back.

And he definitely didn't want to think real hard about how many "firsts" she'd had or hadn't yet had in her life. Because he was supposed to be her boss. And that was supposed to put her out of range of his wholly unprofessional thoughts where she was concerned.

He scrubbed his palm over his jaw. "Fine," he said abruptly. "Go finish your lunch."

"Salvage the lunch, you mean," she muttered. "What if he goes and tells someone you and I are engaged? You're one of the most eligible bachelors in the country. You think news like that won't get out?"

"I don't care if it does. Engagements come and go faster than the seasons."

She blew out a breath. "Maybe in your world," she said before walking back into the restaurant.

Ben's hands curled as he fought the impulse to follow her. To stop the charade with Phillips before it went an inch further.

Instead, he went back upstairs to his suite.

He contacted the concierge to make sure his unfinished beer was billed to his suite.

And then he began pacing again.

But this time it was because—once again—he couldn't get the thought of firsts with Ella out of his head.

Chapter Eight

Ella stood outside the door of Ben's room and drew in a long, steadying breath.

After his entirely unexpected intrusion on her "interview" with Randy, she'd found it nearly impossible to concentrate on anyone but Ben once she'd left him outside the restaurant. She'd returned to the table and done her best to salvage the meeting, but mostly, Randy had only wanted to talk about Ben and his father's meteoric success with Robinson Tech.

She'd come away guiltily confident that the man wanted a chance to work for Robinson Tech.

And he'd also offered, even without being asked, to keep Ella's engagement to Ben confidential.

She almost broke into a sweat just thinking about being engaged to Ben. In fact, she felt so flushed, she pulled off her blazer and folded it over her arm before briskly rapping her knuckles against the door of Ben's room.

He answered it so quickly, she fell back a startled step.

His eyes raked over her from the top of her head to her toes, making her wonder what on earth he was looking for.

Signs that Randy had tried ravishing her in the hotel restaurant?

Her spine stiffened and she met his eyes, though it made her vaguely breathless in the process. "Do you want me to stand here in the hall and tell you what he said?"

He grimaced and stepped out of the doorway so she could enter, and when she heard the door click shut again, she almost wished she *had* remained in the hall.

Her room was luxurious.

His room—well, it was a suite of rooms—was like something out of a movie. She could even see through the windows that it possessed a snow-covered terrace easily as spacious as the room she'd been given.

"Well?"

She looked over her shoulder, realizing her feet had carried her toward those windows. Ben was standing halfway across the room, his arms folded across his chest, making the fine white fabric of his shirt stretch over his shoulders.

The tailored suits he wore were very adept at hiding what she was realizing were very muscular shoulders.

And behind him, through French doors with glass insets, she could see the bedroom, with its very wide bed.

She dragged her eyes away and focused instead on the fan of glossy travel magazines arranged on the coffee table situated in front of a plush, upholstered couch. "His mother met her husband in Colorado Springs, where they were both working as civilians at the US Air Force Academy. I don't know if they met before or after Randy's birth, which also occurred in Colorado Springs." She moistened her lips, feeling Ben's eyes on her like a physical thing. "Randy did say that his maternal grandmother once told him his mother had had an affair with your father when she worked for him in Texas, but he says his mother never confirmed that."

"Assume she did."

"Yes." She dared a quick glance at him, before studying the closest magazine cover featuring a glorious sailboat. "Randy thinks it's pretty funny, considering your supposed interest in hiring him. After your—" she waved her hand "—arrival, he didn't say much else about his family. He was too busy raving over your and your father's achievements. He really has a man crush on your brother, Wes. Says his creative mind is off the charts."

"It is." He unfolded his arms and tugged his tie loose. "Go ahead and say it. I have only myself to blame."

She sucked in her lower lip, not responding.

He tugged his tie loose. "For God's sake, sit. You're making me nervous."

She couldn't imagine him nervous under any circumstances, but she perched gingerly on the edge of the couch, rearranging her blazer on the cushion beside her so she wouldn't get caught ogling her boss.

In the silence of the room, the slither of his tie sounded loud when he pulled it free and tossed it on top of the sailboat magazine. "Did you fess up that there was no job?"

She looked at him then. "Of course not!" She looked away just as quickly, though, when he absently flicked open the top few buttons of his shirt. Heaven help her if she ever saw him shirtless, considering the fluttering going on inside her stomach at the mere glimpse of his bare throat.

She stared fixedly at the sailing magazine, over which his silver tie was draped. "I told him we, um, we had a few more candidates to meet and we would be in touch."

He sank down in the chair opposite her, stretching out his long legs and threading his fingers together across his abdomen. "Fine."

She dared a glance upward as far as his thumbs, which he was pressing together. "Are you? Going to be in touch?"

"Should I be?"

She let out a faint huff. "The point is to find out if he is your brother, isn't it? Or have you decided against that just because you took exception to his behavior toward me?"

He pressed the tips of his thumbs to his chin and studied her for a moment, his hooded expression unreadable. "You think he's worth pursuing?"

For some reason, her stomach tightened. "The time lines seem to point that way. I suppose I could steal his water glass or something after he's drunk from it so you could test his DNA. That's a real thing, isn't it?" She knew she was prattling on, but couldn't seem to stop herself. "And not just something off of television shows?"

He dropped his hands to his abdomen again and leaned his head back against the chair. His eyes were nearly closed, only narrow slits of deep blue visible between his dark lashes. "My last brush with DNA testing had more to do with cheek swabs and saliva than water glasses."

Before she could contemplate that odd statement, his legs jackknifed and he pushed up from the chair in a blur of motion. "Call him back. Set up a meeting here for tomorrow morning."

"Here, here?" She glanced around the suite that his long legs were eating up as he'd begun pacing. "Or here at the hotel?"

He stopped in front of the French doors and pushed them open. "Here," he said, disappearing into the bedroom. He did not close the doors after himself. "Call him now," he instructed. "Phone's on the desk."

She blamed the flood of butterflies in her stomach on the hotel room setting, and retrieved the business card Randy had given her before they'd parted and went over to the desk. "So you're going to meet with him yourself tomorrow," she said loudly while she poked out the numbers on the fancy phone.

"Possibly."

His voice was closer and she looked back to see he'd returned to the living area from the bedroom. And he'd changed from his white shirt into a wheat-colored pullover sweater that looked so rich and soft it was probably cashmere. He'd also exchanged his trousers for faded blue jeans that accentuated his long legs.

"Possibly?" she repeated faintly. He looked as if he'd walked off the cover of the sailboat magazine.

"You'll start off and we'll play it by ear." He went back into the bedroom, which showed her that the rear view of his blue jeans was as excellent as the front view.

She exhaled silently and quickly redialed the number, since her distraction with him had caused a mess of her first attempt.

Randy picked up after only a few rings and she quickly relayed Ben's request for another meeting. They agreed on a time and that was that. She hung up and retrieved her blazer from the couch. "He'll be here at nine," she told Ben when he reappeared in the doorway with the bed behind him.

"Fine. Get changed and meet me in the lobby."

She hesitated. "What's the plan?"

"Getting you an engagement ring, of course."

Her jaw loosened.

His dimple flashed. "You should see your face," he said drily. "I'm kidding. Obviously."

"Obviously," she repeated over the odd ringing inside her ears.

"The city you've never seen awaits. Plus, I need to pick up some chocolate for Bonita from this place on Newbury Street. If I go back to the office without something for her, she'll make my life miserable for a month."

"No, she wouldn't."

"You haven't met her," he said and headed for the door. "Come on. Get moving. Daylight doesn't last long here this time of year."

"It'll only take me a few minutes to change," she assured him, and hurried through the door.

When she was gone, Ben pushed the door closed and silently banged his head against the wood panel a few times.

Having Ella in his hotel suite hadn't been the most brilliant idea he'd ever had. He was in near danger of needing a cold shower. Walking around Boston on a cold winter day would suffice just as well.

He grabbed his overcoat and checked his messages on the elevator ride down to the lobby. The second he showed his face, Serena, the concierge who'd checked them in, approached. He'd dealt with her many times on previous visits. She was one of the best, and even though he'd been tempted often enough over the years to see if she was interested in spending time together outside of her job capacity, he hadn't.

"What can I help you with this afternoon, Mr. Robinson? Tickets for the Celtics game tonight? A comedy group? Symphony?"

"Not this time, Serena. But you can call Johnny for me."

"Right away." She pulled out a small walkie-talkie and spoke into it before tucking it away again in her side pocket.

"Looks like business here is going well. The place is packed." He hadn't been able to book the presidential suite, which was his usual preference. But on short notice, he supposed he couldn't blame them.

"We're gearing up for the wine festival," she said, glancing around the teeming lobby. "When are you going to bring a division of Robinson Tech to Boston?"

He laughed. The question was a long-running one that dated back to before Ben had been appointed COO. "Like I've told you before, you'd have to take that up with my old man."

She smiled brilliantly but Ben barely noticed because he'd caught sight of Ella stepping off the elevator. She'd changed out of the simple blue skirt and white blouse into jeans that hugged her hips and a thick turtleneck that clung to her curvy torso. She'd also pulled her hair down from its braid and it waved, a gleaming, vibrant red, long past her shoulders.

She looked young and carefree and impossibly, irresistibly appealing.

"Ahh," Serena said softly. "I see now what entertainment you're seeking."

He gave her a look rooted in a decade of stays with the hotel when she'd been only a reservation clerk and he an entry-level account manager with Robinson Computers. "Don't you have something more important to do?"

She smiled knowingly. "Nothing is more important than seeing to the comfort of one of our treasured, long-standing guests. Perhaps the usual strawberries and champagne in your suite later?"

He exhaled noisily. There was nothing usual about Ella. "Go away, Serena."

She chuckled and walked away, greeting Ella with a smile as they passed.

Then Ella reached him and began pulling on the black peacoat she'd worn earlier.

And that reminded him... "Serena," he called, and the concierge immediately about-faced and returned to them. "Ms. Thomas needs a scarf and hat to use. We'll be walking a bit, too."

"Certainly." Serena turned to Ella. "Do you have a preference of colors?"

Ella looked bemused. "No, but—"

"Give me three minutes," Serena said, and sailed off again.

Ella looked up at Ben. "She's not going to bill something exorbitant from one of the shops here to my room, is she?" She pulled a pair of bright red knit mittens from her pockets. "Because I've got these and I don't need—"

"She's not going to bill anything to *you*," he promised. He put his hands on her shoulders and turned her so she was looking out the front entrance, where the light snowfall that had begun was visible. "And you do need."

She'd gone stiff and still the second he'd touched her, and he pulled his hands away, swearing inwardly at himself.

"What about you?" She pointedly looked at his bare head. "You're not wearing a hat."

"But I have this." He pulled a short muffler from his pocket and flipped it around his neck, shoving the ends under his turned-up collar. He hadn't even pulled his gloves from his other pocket when Serena returned with a thick, long scarf hanging over her arm and a matching knitted cap. In red that perfectly matched Ella's mittens.

"I had a feeling," she said humorously when she noticed Ella's mittens. "Will these do?"

When Ella hesitated, probably worrying in her accountant-to-be head about costs or consequences, he took the scarf from Serena and twined it around Ella's neck. The vivid color echoed the flush in her cheeks when he was finished. "They'll do well," he answered, and tugged the cap briskly down over Ella's shining hair. "Keep the coffee hot," he told the concierge before taking Ella's elbow and nudging her toward the hotel entrance.

The second they left the building, he heard Ella suck in a breath. "Wow. The air is—"

"Cold. Hence the scarf and hat." He eyed her, trying to

think like a protective boss and not a lustful man. But it was damn hard when her eyes were sparkling blue and her nose was turning pink already from the cold.

His usual driver, Johnny, was just pulling up to the front of the hotel and without waiting, Ben ushered Ella to the car, pulling open the rear door himself. "Don't get out, Johnny." Ella climbed in and he gestured for her to slide across the backseat so he could follow.

"Nothing like a warm spell, eh, Mr. Robinson? Where can I take you in my city on this fine day?"

"Drop us at Newbury Street. We'll walk as long as Ms. Thomas here doesn't turn into a Popsicle."

"Sure thing, sir." Johnny steered the car away from the hotel into the busy afternoon traffic coursing down Atlantic Avenue. "Another stop at the chocolate shop?"

"Johnny's been driving me on every trip to Boston for the past five years," Ben told Ella.

"Six," Johnny quipped from the driver's seat. "I drive Mr. Robinson Senior when he comes to town, too."

"Lucky you," Ben drawled.

"Your pop's an all-right fella," the driver said on a chuckle. "Always treats me right. Same as you, sir. Haven't seen your mother in a while, though. How is Mrs. Robinson these days?"

"She's well, Johnny. I'll tell her you asked."

"Used to have me drive her to the stationer's on Boylston that she liked. She'd give me heck for my driving, though."

As if to prove the reason, he gunned the car between a Mercedes and a big red tour bus, and Ben saw Ella's red mitten latch onto the armrest.

"Snow slows things down a bit." Johnny continued chatting and Ella's eyebrows rose as she gave Ben a look.

She soundlessly mouthed, *Slow?*

Ben grinned. "This is Ms. Thomas's first time in Boston, Johnny."

"That so?" The car whipped around a corner. "Well, then, it's no wonder you wanted the water taxi earlier."

Ben leaned down toward Ella's ear. Trying not to notice her fresh scent was as productive as trying not to breathe, so he didn't bother. "Johnny gets more talkative the later in the day it gets," he murmured.

She turned a little toward him, and pulled in an audible breath when the car swayed again. "Does his driving get better, too?" she whispered and pushed the red cap farther back on her head.

He couldn't help himself. He carefully moved a lock of lustrous hair away from where it had fallen over her eyes. It wasn't as tempting as her full lips, just a few inches from his own, but it was a close second.

And just as foolish, considering the way her eyes widened and clung to his.

"Johnny's as good as it gets." His voice felt oddly strangled. "He's been driving Boston's streets for thirty years."

"Thirty-seven," the man said from the front seat, reminding Ben that the driver still missed nothing. "Longer'n either one of you have been on this beautiful big earth." He gestured to one side toward the snow-covered park they were passing. "There's the Common. You can ice-skate on the frog pond this time of year, if you're interested."

"I've never ice-skated in my life," Ella admitted on a laugh.

She finally turned her head to look out the window, and Ben breathed a little easier.

"It looks beautiful covered in snow," she went on. "I imagine it's really spectacular when it's not."

"Aye, truer words were never spoken," Johnny said and gestured again. "The Public Garden's there. Some folks think they're one and the same, but the Common's a whole lot older. We Bostonians love 'em both, all the same." As he drove, he kept pointing out local points of interest and soon enough, he'd turned onto Newbury Street and worked the luxury car into a minuscule space along the curb. He hopped out with the agility of a man half his age and opened the sidewalk-side door, offering his hand to help Ella from the car.

When Ben joined her, Johnny clapped his bare hands together. "I'll pick you up at the other end of Newbury, then?"

Ben nodded. He figured the driver would while away the time with his usual book of crossword puzzles and the tablet computer Ben had given him on his last visit to Boston. "That'll be good, Johnny. Thanks."

The driver tipped an imaginary cap and climbed back into the car. A second later, he was whipping out into traffic again.

And that left Ella and Ben alone.

Or as alone as they could be while shoppers walked briskly along the sidewalks, despite the snowflakes falling on their heads.

"So." Ella clapped her mitten-covered hands together a few times and tugged her hair free from where it was trapped beneath the thick scarf around her neck. "Where's the chocolate place you need?"

He took her hand and tucked it around his arm. "Watch out for ice," he said, as if that was good enough reason to walk essentially arm in arm down the wide sidewalk. "It's down a little ways. If you see any shops you want to go into before then, just say the word."

She looked bemused as she gestured toward the designer label sign on the store right next to them. "I'm pretty sure the only thing I can afford around here is the air we're breathing."

"It doesn't cost anything to window-shop." He grinned. "At least that's what my little sister Zoe has told me. Ironic, since she's the apple of our father's eyes and has been spoiled more than any of us. I seriously doubt she's ever actually *window*-shopped." Since Ella didn't seem interested in approaching the store, he began walking. Sooner or later, they'd be bound to encounter something that sparked her interest.

"How many years are between you and the rest of them?"

"A few minutes between me and Wes."

Her nose wrinkled a little as she displayed her winsome, toothy smile. "And the others?"

"Sophie's the youngest at twenty-two. The rest of us are sprinkled in between."

"Eight kids in eleven years. It still boggles my mind. It must have been chaos in your house growing up."

"Not really." He thought about the size of the Robinson estate. "If you tried, you could go days without running into someone else."

She looked up at him, dashing a snowflake away from her eyelashes. "Did you try?"

"A few times." He stepped closer to her to allow a jogger more room as he ran past. "Then I went off to college and when I finished, I never moved back in. I certainly never missed the place, that's for sure."

She looked as if she wanted to say something, but instead, she tugged a little on his arm as she headed closer to the windows of the art gallery they were nearing. She angled her head and studied the multiarmed metal structure in virulent green that was the lone piece displayed in the window. "What do you suppose that's supposed to represent?"

"Hard to say. A morning-after hangover?"

She chuckled and shook her head, continuing on.

"Could also be my mother's feelings where my father is concerned," he added.

She looked up at him again through her lashes. "They've been married a long time."

"Thirty-five years."

Her steps slowed again as they passed a nail salon, but she wasn't looking in the windows. She was still looking at Ben. "Do you think she knew about, ah—"

"His affairs? She'd have to be deaf, dumb and blind not to know. And my mother is none of those things."

"She must be very devoted to him."

"I gave up a long time ago trying to figure out the dynamics of their marriage."

"A marriage that still produced eight children," she pointed out. "Obviously *something* works between them."

"Yeah, but thinking about my parents' sex life isn't something I want to spend too much time doing," he said drily.

"But you're following up on the results of your father's sex life," she countered. "I mean, obviously I'm benefiting, considering what you're paying me, but I still think all of this must be very difficult for you." She stopped and pulled her arm away from his, turning to face him. "I understand what you said before—about everyone deserving to know their roots and the importance of truth and all that—but there's a cost to you, too."

"You haven't been noticing very well that *cost* isn't something I worry too much about."

Her chin went up a notch. "I notice that your voice goes all smooth like it just did when you don't want to talk about something." She gave him a small smile and took several steps up the sidewalk until she reached another window—this one baying out in a half moon that was filled with featureless mannequins wearing summery dresses. "Always seems so strange to me that the clothes being promoted like this never match the season when a person is buying them."

He studied the back of her red-capped head and the thick, glossy hair streaming down her shoulders. "Yes, there's a cost," he said abruptly. "For the most part, at best, my brothers and sisters are pissed that I'm pursuing it. At worst, they're downright furious." His sister Zoe in particular thought he'd gone out of his tree. But then Zoe was their father's favorite and they all knew it.

Ella turned to face him, her expressive eyes looking soft. "But the truth is more important than their feelings?"

"The truth is everything. You said yourself you'd choose truth even over your desire for security."

"Yes, but—" She shook her head and surprised the hell out of him when she tucked her hand once more around his arm, sending something warm through his chest. "The way I see it, you have two issues here. Your father's original identity."

"His *real* identity."

"In your opinion." Her tone was reasonable. "A man in your father's position, I'd think he must have had good reason to remake himself and leave Jerome Fortune behind. Isn't it possible that he considers Gerald Robinson to be his *real* identity?"

Somehow, Ben found his footsteps falling in line with hers as she led the way along the increasingly snowy sidewalk. "He can be whoever the hell he wants to be. But there's no excuse good enough for lying to us about who he was."

"I've never been in your position, so I'm in no position to disagree. But, anyway, that's one issue. Finding any children he might have had outside of his marriage with your mother is the other issue. And it doesn't have anything to do with whether or not he is Jerome Fortune."

"What's your point, Ella?"

"I'm not sure I know what my point is." Her steps slowed again. "But hasn't there ever been something in your life that you'd rather not share with anyone else? Something so intensely private it's nobody's business but your own?"

Henry.

Once Stephanie had reappeared in Ben's life with the blond-haired toddler in tow, he hadn't tried to keep the boy secret. But since she'd taken him away again, he had no desire to bare his feelings about the matter.

Not with his family.

Not with Ella.

"My father is driven and abrupt and temperamental," he said instead. "He's built a business that employs thousands. But he's been lying to his own family our entire lives. Just because he provided for us doesn't mean he was a good father. It sure in hell doesn't mean he's been a good husband.

"There aren't two issues, Ella. There's only one. His lying. And if I accomplish nothing else, it's going to be that it all stops. I'm *not* going to be like him!"

He didn't even realize that he'd started walking faster, practically dragging Ella along with him, until her tennis shoe slid on a patch of ice lurking beneath the thin layer of snow.

He caught her beneath her arm before her foot went completely out from under her and even through her mittens, her fingers latched around his arms. Her lips were way, way too close. All he'd have to do was lower his head—

He pulled the emergency brake on the thought. "Are you all right?"

She didn't answer the question, though. Just posed one of her own. "Is that the real problem you're trying to solve, Ben?" Her voice was breathless. "That you're afraid you're just like your father?"

Chapter Nine

She felt him go rigid, and for a long moment, Ella feared she'd gone too far.

Then the sudden storm clouds faded from Ben's eyes and his voice turned smooth again. "I am like my father. Always have been. Something a nice girl like you would do well to remember."

Even through her mittens and his overcoat, she could feel the tension in his muscles. "That sounds like a warning."

"I said you were intelligent from the get-go."

She moistened her lips, even though doing so just made them colder. "I felt a lot safer with Randy's flirting than I do right now." She could not fathom the insanity that made her admit it aloud. Maybe it was the way she couldn't drag her eyes away from his.

"Much as I disliked seeing him flirt with you, you were definitely safer."

Her chest felt so tight it was hard to breathe. She imagined she could see her own reflection inside his eyes. "Ben—"

He took a step back and pulled her hand once more through his crooked arm. "It's getting cold standing here, and Bonita's chocolates are waiting."

She figured that the famed street would be spectacularly beautiful during warmer months. And it wasn't without charm now, with snowflakes drifting around them, dusting the buildings and the snow-plowed street with a fresh coat of white.

Maybe someday she'd visit Boston while the trees were green and the flowers were in bloom.

But now she was here with Ben.

She exhaled and fell into step with him again.

They eventually reached the chocolatier's shop, which was set down a short staircase from the street level and was smaller inside than she'd envisioned. But the very air was sinfully redolent of chocolate confections and she couldn't help but admire the beautiful displays behind the glass-fronted cases. "I'm gaining weight just looking."

A woman wearing a pristine white apron and a black bow tie appeared and Ben gestured at one of the larger boxes on display. "Give me one of that size and fill it with anything chocolate that has a nut in it. It's for my secretary and she doesn't touch chocolate without nuts. Nothing fruity, either."

The clerk plucked an empty box from under her counter and tucked shimmery white tissue paper in it before deftly beginning to fill it with chocolates of every size and shape.

"Your secretary is a lucky woman," Ella said drily, because she'd noticed the tastefully discreet prices listed under the confections.

"Indeed, she is," the clerk agreed. She stopped near Ella to select several glossy rounds topped with walnut halves. "Would you like a sample of anything?"

"Oh." Ella shook her head. "I couldn't."

"Sure, she could." Ben stepped next to her, touching her shoulder as he leaned over to examine the displays.

"Your husband is right." The clerk's hand hovered over the trays of precisely arranged chocolates. "Perhaps a white ganache or an almond praline?"

Ella opened her mouth to correct the clerk, but Ben's hand moved to the back of her neck, scorching even through the scarf, and the words caught in her throat.

"Give her one of those Manhattan truffles."

She almost did a double take at the quick wink he gave her. Instead, she just felt heat course down through the rest of her from the source at the back of her neck, and when the clerk set a silver foil cup containing a glossy round truffle on top of the glass, she quickly sank her teeth into it, biting off half.

Dark, heady chocolate dissolved blissfully on her tongue, but it was nothing compared to having Ben slip the other half of the truffle out of her fingers and pop it into his mouth.

She actually felt faint and considered tearing off her coat to run into the snowy outdoors for relief.

"There's a first," Ben murmured. "Our first whiskey truffle together."

The clerk fit the lid in place on Bonita's chocolates before sliding the box toward Ben across the glass. "You sound like newlyweds," she said with a benevolent smile. "I can always spot the newlyweds. Can I get you anything else?"

"Pack up a dozen of these." He flicked the empty foil cup and slid a credit card toward her in exchange.

"My pleasure." The clerk took the card and greeted a customer who entered behind them before moving toward her cash register.

Ben's hand fell away from Ella's neck and she moved

near the door, where she had a slim hope of catching her breath while he finished paying for his purchases.

The snow was falling even harder when they went up the short flight of stairs to reach the street level. "Why did you let her think we were married?"

"It's the theme for the day, evidently."

"Yes. Karma for you lying to Randy about being my fiancé."

She was grateful to see Johnny and his car waiting at the curb and aimed straight for it.

The driver opened the door for her and she ducked her head and climbed in, sliding across the seat for Ben to follow. Then she sat forward to offer Johnny one of her Manhattan truffles once he closed the door after Ben and got back behind the wheel.

"Don't mind if I do, miss." He plucked a round truffle from the small box and popped it in his mouth before pulling out into the traffic that hadn't lessened a speck despite the snowfall. "Back to the hotel, sir?"

"I thought we'd hit Little Italy for dinner, but it's still early."

"Already be a line forming outside of Giacomo's," Johnny said. "Always is."

Ella pulled off her mittens and unwound her scarf, since the car interior was toasty warm and she still felt like she was burning up from the inside. "What's Giacomo's?"

"Best Italian joint in the North End." Ben set the large bag containing Bonita's chocolates on the seat between them while he pulled out his cell phone and studied it. "They don't take reservations and there's hardly any space inside, but it's worth the wait every time." He returned his phone to his pocket, then pulled open his coat and dropped his scarf in the bag with the box of candy. "Give Ms. Thomas the city tour, Johnny. And turn down the heater. We're roasting back here."

Ella couldn't help but wish that the cause of his over-heating had less to do with the Town Car's heater and more to do with her.

At least then he'd be sharing her similar discomfort.

The warm air blowing from the heating vents disappeared and Johnny launched into his role again as tour guide as he drove through the city, pointing out landmarks, some famous and some so obscure she felt almost certain he was pulling her leg. He ended in the North End, dropping them off again at Ben's request on Hanover Street in front of the restaurant, where a line of people stood outside on the sidewalk, not seeming to care about the weather as they waited.

It took the better part of an hour, but eventually it was their turn to weave their way through the closely set tables crowded inside the small restaurant. They sat at a table for four with two strangers and Ella's bemusement only increased from there. Wine. Seafood. Pasta. It was loud and noisy and delicious and so close that Ben's knees were pressed against hers beneath the table the entire while.

And for the first time since she'd met him what seemed so much longer than a mere week ago, he seemed to actually relax, not checking his phone the entire time.

After the filling meal, she expected Ben would want to return to the hotel, but again he surprised her, choosing to walk to a nearby pastry shop, where he insisted she try a cannoli. And even though she was positively stuffed, she managed to consume half of the delicious cream-filled dessert before begging off. "I'm going to explode," she told him plaintively, "if you keep feeding me like this."

He smiled and finished the cannoli the same way he had her chocolate truffle. Then he pulled her out of the pastry shop and down the street a few more doors and into a dimly lit pub, where she sat on a high bar stool at the crowded bar and Ben stood so close beside her that she felt engulfed by him.

It was more intoxicating than the wine, the food and the desserts could ever be.

When the bartender approached, Ben settled his hand on her shoulder and leaned over her so closely she felt his chest against her back. "What would you like?"

She looked up at him. His face was so close, she could see a faint starburst pattern in his blue irises, and she barely managed to repress the *you* that immediately rose to her lips. Instead, she cleared her throat slightly. "What, uh, whatever you're having."

His gaze dropped to her lips for a moment so brief, she was afraid she'd imagined it, before he spoke to the bartender. "Cognac for me. Mineral water for the lady." He shot her a quick smile. "Don't want to be responsible for a hangover on your part come tomorrow morning."

She forced a little smile.

Just because she was losing her head, didn't mean he was. "Prudent."

When they finally climbed into the rear of the Town Car and Johnny dropped them off in front of the hotel, it was after midnight.

"Thank you, Johnny," she said when he opened the car door for her yet again. "I feel like I had a personal tour guide."

He beamed. "My pleasure, miss."

Ben shook the driver's hand and Ella couldn't help but wonder if there'd been an exchange of cash in the action. The snow had stopped falling when they'd had their dinner, but now the night was even colder, an icy wind cutting easily through her layers, and she quickly went inside the hotel.

At this time of the night, the gloriously beautiful lobby

was nearly deserted and when Ben pressed the call button
for the elevator, the doors slid open immediately.

Feeling unaccountably edgy, she pushed the button for
her floor and moved to the back of the car, leaning against
the wall. He might be able to put aside the things they'd
said on the street outside of the chocolatier's, but she wasn't
finding it so easy.

Ben hit the button for his own floor and the doors glided
shut, closing them in alone. "Tired?"

What she felt was wired. And he was the single cause
of it. But she shrugged her shoulders, leaving him to interpret it however he chose. "Johnny should have been
tired. But he didn't seemed to be. I hope he gets paid well
by the hotel."

"He doesn't work for the hotel. He has his own business.
Employs ten other drivers the last time I asked."

"Impressive." She looked at the floor display. The elevator seemed to be crawling and even though they had
the entire car to themselves, Ben had chosen to lean in the
corner less than a foot away from her, his hands stretched
out against the rail that ran the perimeter. The glossy shopping bag from the chocolate shop hung from his thumb
that he tapped slowly against the rail. The rustling the bag
made as it swayed sounded loud, but not as loud as the
thumping inside her chest. "Thank you for dinner and…
and everything."

He inclined his head slightly, his eyes typically unreadable. "Now you can say you've seen at least a bit of
Boston."

"Yes." She stared down at the carpeted floor and moistened her lips, wishing the elevator would hurry up. When
the doors dinged softly a moment later, she automatically
stepped forward, only to feel Ben's hand clasp her arm.

Her eyes flew to his face, but he was looking at the elevator doors and she realized they were opening to admit

more hotel guests and they hadn't reached her floor yet at all.

She subsided, and Ben tugged her even closer when the elevator continued to fill with the increasingly boisterous group until her back was pressed against his chest as she stood directly in front of him, his hand on her waist through her coat.

She stood stock-still, even though she had the worst desire to sink back into him.

The other guests were clearly celebrating and they tumbled out again a few floors later. Alone again, Ella had no reason to remain plastered against Ben and she gave him a smile that felt awkward and tight as she stepped away. "Looks like they were having a good time."

His eyes were hooded again. "You don't have to be afraid of me, Ella."

She started. "I'm not afraid of you!" She looked at the floor numbers again. She felt like an absolute idiot and didn't like it one bit. "Maybe *you* should be afraid of me," she muttered, proving that she was nevertheless still fueled by too much wine, sugar and the intoxication of *him*.

Before he could respond—if he even wanted or intended to—the elevator stopped again, this time at her floor, and the moment the doors opened, she stepped off. "Good night, Ben."

Then the doors closed again and Ella's shoulders slumped.

She hauled in a deep breath and made her way to her room on legs that felt like mush.

Ella presented herself at Ben's suite the next morning exactly two minutes before nine. She wore her navy blue skirt once again, this time with a silky white tee, and she left the blazer behind.

Ben answered her knock and seemed to be back in his usual mode, with his cell phone at his ear with one hand

and a newspaper in his other. He gestured at the dining table in his living area. "Breakfast. Help yourself."

She didn't have to ask if Randy was already there; she could see for herself that he was not. She crossed the room and studied the breakfast selection laid out on the sideboard. Ben had enough food there to feed a dozen people, and she filled a plate with fluffy scrambled eggs, two slices of crispy bacon and a blueberry muffin of decadent proportions. Then she sat at one end of the gleaming table and tucked in.

She felt famished and blamed it on fruitlessly chasing Ben through her dreams all night long. It was just as well that he didn't join her at the table. Instead he paced around the living area as he made one call after another, clearly conducting business as usual even from a distance. She hadn't finished even half of her food when they heard a knock on the door.

Ben gave her a look and went into the adjoining room, pulling the doors closed.

She huffed out a breath, trying to rid herself of her nervousness and crossed the room to open the door. "Good morning, Randy."

Even though it was a Saturday, he was dressed in a dark suit and tie every bit as professional as Ben's. But unlike every time she looked at her handsome boss, the effect from Randy was totally wasted on her. She invited him in, gesturing at the breakfast spread across the room. "I hope you're hungry. Mr. Robinson has a small feast here."

Randy's gaze was frankly curious as he entered the suite and looked around. "Is he here?"

She didn't want to lie outright, even though this entire exercise was based on pretense. "He's on a call," she said. "He'll join us if he is able." She led the way to the dining area. "Can I pour you a coffee or some juice?"

He glanced toward her plate. "Is that your breakfast? Finish eating. I can pour my own coffee."

He seemed insistent, so she returned to her seat and a moment later, he joined her, sitting opposite her. "Pretty sweet suite you've got here," he said cheerfully as he tucked in to his own breakfast.

He probably figured she'd shared the room with her "fiancé," and even though she hadn't, she still felt her face warm. "Yes, it's very nice. Thank you for coming again. I hope it wasn't too inconvenient."

His lips twitched. "Nothing's too inconvenient when it comes to Robinson Tech."

Her conscience nipped again and she rose to refill her own coffee cup. "Do you live near here?"

"My folks have a place in Back Bay. Too high rent for me, though," he added ruefully. "I have an apartment in Watertown."

With that door opened so conveniently, Ella sat down again and cradled the china cup between both hands. "Do you have any brothers or sisters?"

He shook his head. "Mom always said she wanted more kids, but she had a lot of trouble carrying me."

"That's too bad."

He nodded around a mouthful of toast that he chased with coffee. "I was born really prematurely," he said eventually. "Just twenty-six weeks. I spent the first four months of my life in the hospital."

She hid her dismay. Even before Antonia had left Robinson Computers, Gerald had left the country on a business trip. Ben's notes about his father's schedule and whereabouts during those years had been carefully reconstructed. If Randy had been born several months early, there was no possible way that Gerald Robinson could have fathered him. Not when he and Antonia were in different parts of the world when their child would have been con-

ceived. "Well, I'm glad things turned out okay for you,"
she said. "My, um, my little brother was also premature,"
she confided. "He has cerebral palsy."

"That's gotta be tough."

"It's a concern, of course, but Rory's the tough one.
He's overcome a lot. Mostly his CP affects his legs." She
smiled. "He wants to design computers someday."

"Then you're marrying into the right family."

Ella laughed because he expected it. She took a few more
sips of coffee, then excused herself and went to find Ben.

He was in the bedroom, sitting at a desk near the windows with another view of the outdoor terrace. The newspaper was unfolded on top of the desk and his cell phone
was sitting on top of that. But she had the distinct impres-
sion that he'd been staring out the terrace when she'd interrupted.

She kept her eyes diligently away from his unmade
bed, but it was difficult. "He's not your brother." She kept
her voice low, even though she'd pulled the doors closed
after her.

"How do you know?"

She relayed the information. "There's no way he could
have been conceived when his mother was still interning
for your father. The dates are just too far out of line, knowing he was so premature."

"Maybe he wasn't early. Nearly thirty years ago? Babies
were regularly claimed as 'premature' to explain away a
birth that came a little too soon after a wedding."

"I'll see if I can find the hospital records. A long hospital stay like he's described is more than just glossing over
a baby made a few weeks before the *I do*s. Which there
weren't, anyway, not right away. Even though Randy says
his mother and Ronald Phillips met in Colorado Springs,
don't forget that I couldn't find any record of their marriage until they moved to Massachusetts years and years

later. I don't know whether or not Ronald is his natural father, but for your purpose, it's not important, anyway. What *is* important is that Gerald *isn't*."

He scrubbed his hand down his face before he reached out and grabbed his phone. But all he did was tap the edge of it against the newspaper-covered desk. "Fine."

She wasn't sure if he was dismissing her or not. "What should I tell him now? The poor guy thinks he's got a crack at working for Robinson Tech."

"Tell him the job requires relocating. Maybe he'll lose interest."

Ella shook her head. "He won't." But she left the bedroom, leaving the doors closed again. She rejoined Randy at the dining table and picked up the fancy, silver coffee server. "More?"

"Sure." He held out his cup and she refilled it before topping off her own. "Do you mind if I ask how many other candidates you're considering?"

"Three." It was appalling how quickly she came up with answers, but that was the number of individuals currently on her latest list of baby-mama suspects. "I do need to tell you that relocation would be necessary. Is that—"

"Not a problem," Randy assured her.

"Right." She started to sit when she noticed the French doors opening again and Ben appeared.

Randy noticed, too, and immediately stood, extending his hand. "Mr. Robinson. Good to see you again."

Ben gestured at the food. "I hope you helped take care of getting rid of some of this stuff."

Randy grinned. "My starving-student days are still fresh in my mind. I try not to pass up too many meals that are offered to me."

"You've got an impressive résumé. And Lester Tomlinson speaks highly of you."

"He's BRD's vice president." Randy looked surprised.

"I know." Ben's gaze traveled over Ella for a moment before returning to Randy. He pulled a card from his lapel pocket and handed it to the younger man. "Give my secretary, Bonita, a call on Monday. We'll set you up to come to Austin. Get a close-up look at what we've got to offer you."

Randy eagerly took the card and he smiled brilliantly at Ella. "Thank *you*!"

Ben looked vaguely amused before he walked Randy toward the door of the suite. "Might want to save the thanks, once you find out working for Robinson Tech is more of a calling than a job."

Randy's smile didn't lose a watt. "I'm up to the challenge, I promise."

Ella sat down at the table, cradling her coffee, and waited until Ben returned once Randy was gone.

He gave her a glance before pouring himself a cup. "What are you looking at me like that for?"

Warmth bloomed inside her chest as she watched him. "You're a softy," she said. "You're going to give him a job."

"We give lots of people jobs," he said drily. He plucked a slice of bacon from the heated dish and ate it with his fingers. "Even more jobs with our latest expansion. I am *not* a softy."

He was acting as if he hadn't done anything at all out of the ordinary. When she knew just how far from ordinary this situation had been. "Actually *giving* him a job had never been part of your plan."

"Plans change. Aside from trying to flirt with my HR rep, he's got skills."

"You're not worried he'll go around telling people you're engaged to me?"

"I'll make sure he won't." He sounded unconcerned and polished off the bacon slice before wiping his fingers on a napkin. "So Randy's off the list. Who's next? Someone in Chicago, you said?"

She scrambled a little to keep up with the sudden shift. "Uh, yes. Chicago. Nancy Belgard."

"She was with the advertising firm my father once used."

"Yes. I have the notes in my room if you want to go over them."

He shook his head, glancing at his watch. "Later."

She immediately rose and moved the used plates to the sideboard. The food she and Randy had eaten hadn't made a dent in the generous buffet. "It'll only take me a few minutes to get ready to leave for the airport."

"A commendable trait, considering my experience with my sisters. But we don't have to race back to Austin all that fast. The sky's clear and there's still plenty of the city that you haven't yet seen. Not to mention Cambridge. And your water-taxi ride, of course."

He hadn't said a word the night before about more sightseeing. "That's very generous of you, but—"

"I'm not generous, Ella. I'm selfish. I want what I want when I want it."

She watched him over her coffee cup as she took a long sip. It *was* really good coffee.

When she was finished, she set the empty cup next to the used plates. "Saying something doesn't make it so, Ben," she said as she headed for the door. "So far, the only selfish thing I've seen you do was eat the other half of my truffle yesterday. But if you selfishly want to show me more of this fabulous city, I suppose I can suck it up and go along." Smiling impudently, she pulled open the door, only to gasp when he followed her and reached above her head to push it shut again.

"I *am* selfish," he said flatly and planted his mouth on hers.

Chapter Ten

Ella went rigid with shock.

For about a millisecond.

Then sensation exploded in her veins like a Texas wildfire and she rushed headlong into it. Her hands gripped the lapels of his jacket as she sprang up on her toes, and he slid an arm around her back, arching her even higher against him while his kiss devoured her.

She'd never before believed a kiss could cause fireworks. The one guy she'd ever slept with—a fellow accounting student—had seemed perfectly satisfactory up until that very moment.

Because a kiss *could* cause fireworks.

Ben's kiss.

The colors weren't just bursting to life inside her head. They were igniting in every cell. And then she felt his hot palm sliding beneath her shirt, climbing up her spine, and she was shocked at the moan that rose in her throat and the need that sank through her.

Then she felt his other hand wrapping in her ponytail and he pulled his mouth from hers, breathing harshly. His eyes weren't inscrutable now. They were lit with an unholy blue fire. And they were singeing every inch of her face as he looked at her.

This wasn't flirting.

This was want. Pure and hot and inescapable.

And recognizing it made her shudder.

"I don't sleep with people who work for me." His voice was rough, abrading her senses.

"Are you firing me?"

"I don't fire people who don't sleep with me, either."

"I didn't think you did." She stared at his lips while her own tingled. She was excruciatingly aware of his hand against her bare flesh and the fact that his bed was about twenty steps away.

"I told you that you were safer with Phillips's flirting."

Her breasts were crushed against the breadth of his hard chest. She wasn't sure if it was her own heart beating so hard or if it was his. "Do you want to sleep with me, Ben?" She already could feel the answer to that pressing hard and insistently against her abdomen.

He let out a short, strangled laugh. "Yes." He pressed his mouth to her forehead. Then exhaled. "No. Because I don't want to ruin things."

She was finding it difficult to keep her eyes open. She let go of one crushed lapel and ran her fingers over his tight jaw. "Ruin what things?" Her fingertips crept slowly into his dark hair. The strands were thick and silky.

His hand left her spine and he grabbed her hand, stilling her progress. He pressed his open mouth to her palm and she swallowed hard.

Then he was stepping away from her, releasing her hand. Her ponytail.

Only a few inches, but the distance might as well have been a mile.

"Ruin everything." His voice had turned flat. "I'm sorry. I crossed a line I promised myself I wouldn't cross."

"I'm not sorry." She was incapable of preventing the admission.

"You would have been." He turned away from her and cupped his hand around the back of his neck.

His knuckles were white.

An ache formed deep inside her that had nothing to do with unquenched desire. "Ben."

He didn't look at her, but his hand dropped.

"It's okay," she said softly. "If you're going to beat yourself up over something, please don't let it be for this. I'm a big girl. We kissed. It's not a crime, so forget about it. I will." She fumbled for the doorknob behind her and pulled open the door. "I'm going to change. We can meet in the lobby and sightsee. Or we can go home. Your call. Either way, I'm still going to be okay. I'm not going to quit helping you."

"Because you want your college education paid for."

"Yes." Her palm was sweaty on the knob. "And because I want to help you. Because it's important to you."

His shoulders rose and fell in an enormous sigh. "Don't forget the scarf and hat," he said after a moment. "It'll be even colder out on the water."

She chewed the inside of her cheek, hesitating. He still hadn't turned to look at her. "I'll meet you in the lobby." It was clearly a safer setting for them.

He didn't answer. Just nodded and pulled out his cell phone when it pinged softly. "Bonita," he said into it. "Yeah, I know it's Saturday. That's why you get the ridiculous salary you get—"

Ella shakily stepped out of the suite, pulling the door closed behind her.

When she thought she could walk to the elevator without having her legs collapse from underneath her, she went down to her own room.

She exchanged her skirt and high-heeled pumps again for her jeans and tennis shoes. She'd already showered earlier that morning and she swept up her meager supply of cosmetics, and the fancy little tubes and bottles provided by the hotel into her zippered case and dropped it in her satchel, along with the rest of her clothes. She dumped her taxation book on top. At the rate she was going, she wasn't going to have much of it read at all before her class started. With the satchel ready to go, she left it by the door. She tucked her flat wallet and room key in her front jeans pocket, grabbed her coat and the hat and scarf, and went downstairs to the lobby.

The place was more crowded with pleasure travelers than it had been the day before. There were still a number of comfortable chairs available, but she was too keyed up to sit and wait for Ben, so she wandered around while keeping an eye out on the elevators for sight of him.

Her watch told her a full thirty minutes had passed before he finally appeared. She saw immediately that he hadn't changed out of his business suit. The afternoon before had been the only time she'd seen him in more casual clothes, but she couldn't help wonder if his choice now had anything to do with that kiss.

Was he trying to emphasize his boss-ly position?

She caught sight of her reflection in a window and made a face at herself. More likely, Ben was just being Ben. Sexual attraction clearly wasn't going to push him off his usual course.

Determined to prove that the same could be said of herself, she crossed the lobby to intercept him. "Aren't you going to need your overcoat?" she asked when she reached him. He didn't have the coat with him at all.

He held up his cell phone. "Something's come up that I need to take care of."

Disappointment coursed through her but she did her best to hide it. "Okay. My bag is packed. All I need to do is grab it."

He shook his head and touched the small of her back, directing her inexorably toward the hotel entrance. "Johnny's going to finish giving you a tour. I'll meet you as soon as I'm able."

She swallowed the protest that she'd rather wait for him and let herself be ushered outside where Johnny was once again waiting with the Town Car. With her evidently passed into the capable hands of the driver, Ben went back inside the hotel. Before the door closed behind him, he was once again talking on his cell phone.

"Boy works as hard as his papa," Johnny said, pulling open the rear door for her.

"Could I sit in front with you?"

The gray-haired man smiled. "Aye, sure." He pushed the rear door closed and opened the passenger door instead. "Don't often have such a pretty girl sitting beside me."

"How many times have you kissed the Blarney Stone, Johnny?"

He chuckled and waited until she was stowed inside before closing the door and rounding the vehicle to get behind the wheel. "So, miss. What's your pleasure today?"

Ben, she thought longingly.

And fruitlessly.

She pinned a smile on her face and focused on the genial driver. "Anywhere you choose. You're the expert."

"Right you are, then." He pulled away from the hotel, avoiding a crew that was in the process of removing holiday wreaths from the light poles. "You know, for a while in the 1600s, celebrating Christmas was outlawed in Boston…"

* * *

It was late afternoon before Johnny deposited Ella at the wharf, where a water taxi was waiting.

"Just walk on down those steps," the driver said, gesturing. "Mr. Robinson should be there already."

"Thanks, Johnny." Ella impulsively reached up to kiss the driver's cheek. She hadn't been able to spend the day sightseeing with Ben, but she still had enjoyed herself. She couldn't have done otherwise, considering Johnny's engaging knowledge about "his" city.

The man smiled and patted her shoulder before nudging her toward the brick sidewalk leading to the steps. "You be sure and call on me when you come back to Boston."

Ella smiled back and waved as she walked away, though she figured it was pretty unlikely she'd make it back to the beautiful city. Not anytime soon, anyway. And she would never be able to afford to hire a private driver like Johnny. "Drive carefully," she called back before she began down the steps.

There was a small line of people formed at the base and Ben's head topped them all.

Butterflies flitted around inside her tummy at the sight of him, and when he turned his head and noticed her, they broke into a downright frenzy. He stepped out of line and she saw that he was carrying her satchel again the same way he had when they'd left Texas.

"Sorry I didn't have a chance to meet up with you earlier," he said.

The stiff wind tugging at her ponytail below her knit cap was also flirting with his dark hair, tumbling it over his forehead, seeming to subtract years and responsibility. "That's okay. You've probably seen it all dozens of times over already."

"Not with you, I haven't."

The words made her feel warm inside, even though common sense warned her against putting too much faith in them.

A long water taxi sat alongside the dock and the people at the head of the line were beginning to board. "You really didn't have to do this," she said, gesturing at the boat. "Johnny could have driven us back to the airport just as easily."

"And have you miss out on the full experience?" He shook his head and fell into line behind a young woman with two small children.

"You know it's a shuttle bus that will pick us up on the other side of the harbor and take us to the airport," she warned. "Johnny told me all about it." Along with a bushel of other trivia.

Ben's lips twitched. "I know."

"And you're okay with that? Riding a shuttle."

"I'm not *that* spoiled," he drawled. He reached down to help lift one of the kids ahead of them over the edge of the boat and the tot's mom sent him a grateful smile. Then he turned and held Ella's hand until she'd crossed, as well, and stepped down onto the boat that was rocking steeply in the windswept water.

She retrieved her mitten-clad hand as soon as she could and balled it up inside her pocket. The water taxi had an enclosed cabin where most of the people were heading, but Ella hung back. Ben seemed to have no objection, either.

They were the last to board, and the boat pilot chattered as he walked through the area, briskly collecting tickets and issuing instructions.

Ella sat down on one of the padded seats lining the perimeter of the boat and stared back at the wharf as the boat moved away from it.

Ben dumped her satchel and his garment bag on the

bench between them and sat down, too, stretching out his long legs in front of him.

She'd assured him that she would forget about the kiss. But she'd lied. Forgetting it would be as easy as forgetting her own name. So unless she was somehow stricken with a freak case of amnesia, she was afraid she was stuck with the memory.

The little girl he'd helped into the boat started trotting back and forth from beneath the covered canopy to where they were sitting and Ella smiled at her.

"Think you'll want kids someday?"

Ben's abrupt question made her start. She looked at him, but he was watching the child.

"I haven't thought much about it," she said truthfully. "I suppose someday. After my degree. After—" She shrugged.

"After you establish yourself?"

She nodded.

His lips twisted a little.

"What about you," she asked casually. "Do you want to be a father? A husband?" She was proud of her humorous smile. "A real one, I mean."

"I thought I was a father for nearly a year."

Her falsely humorous smile faded. She studied his solemn profile as he studied the little girl's antics. She easily recalled the snapshot of a blond child she'd inadvertently found in Ben's desk. Of the child's room at his home. The cheerful trains and the beautiful crib.

She'd thought it felt unused.

But now *deserted* seemed more apt.

"What happened?"

Ben's shoulders moved restlessly. "His real father staked his claim and took him away."

She waited for more, but nothing seemed forthcoming. She touched his sleeve. "I'm sorry."

"He's better off."

"What's his name?"

"Henry." He finally looked from the little girl to Ella. "His mother, Stephanie, told me he was mine. We'd been… involved. I believed her. Until Henry's real father had a DNA test done that proved otherwise."

Questions about Stephanie clamored inside her. She resolutely ignored them. "Did he live with you?"

He nodded. "Ten months. His mother, too."

Ella swallowed. Had Stephanie used the lovely room next door to the nursery? Or had she and Ben really *lived* together? As a couple? Had he loved her? Did he still? "When is the last time you saw Henry?"

"Six months ago."

Puzzle pieces shifted around and began falling into place.

"They moved to California," he went on, his voice flat. "Henry's not even three years old. He won't remember me."

But Ben would remember Henry.

Her eyes suddenly stung.

Without realizing she did so, she slid her mitten down his sleeve and curled her fingers around his hand. "I'm so sorry." No wonder it was so important for him to find out if he had other brothers and sisters.

Ben's hand turned upward and squeezed hers back.

A few minutes later, the boat reached the other side of the harbor and docked. Ben let go of Ella's hand and took up their baggage, and they left the water taxi behind.

When they reached the top of the ramp at street level, she looked back across the water. She could see the distinctive arch of the hotel.

"Shuttle's here," Ben said, drawing her attention.

She looked away from the hotel and followed him to the bus.

They flew back on a plane very similar to the first one. They'd been in the air nearly an hour when Ella pulled out her notes on Nancy Belgard and showed them to him. "Her name's Nancy Sylvester now. She had a daughter twenty-five years ago. Sierra. I haven't been able to trace Sierra, but that's Nancy's current address in Chicago." She flipped to another page in her notebook. "I also have Constance Ray, who worked briefly as one of your dad's secretaries. Near as I can tell, she moved to Montreal about twenty years ago, shortly after she stopped working for him. She has three kids and the youngest—a girl, also— is about the right age."

"Any others?"

She flipped the notebook page again. "London. An architect there named Keaton Whitfield." She hesitated for a moment, but then decided there was no point in hiding the detail. It was crucial, after all. "He's a few months younger than you and Wes," she continued evenly and pretended not to notice the grimace he gave. "If the number of mentions of him on the internet is any indication, he seems to be fairly well known. His mother's on the list you gave me." She handed Ben the notebook so he could look for himself.

He flipped slowly through the pages. "Hope your passport is up-to-date."

"Passport!" She couldn't help but laugh. "When would I have had need for a passport?"

He gave her a chagrined look. "Right. You've only been to Seattle and San Francisco."

"Even if I did have a passport, I wouldn't go overseas. Not to London, if that's what you're thinking."

"It was." He set aside the notebook and focused on her. "Why wouldn't you want to go? If things get that far? Judging by your reaction to Boston, you obviously like traveling to new places."

She liked traveling with *Ben*.

Telling him that was out of the question, though. "My

brother has cerebral palsy," she said. "With my mom's work schedule, it's tough on them if I have to be gone for too long."

Comprehension crossed his face. "That's why you hesitated to come to Boston? Why didn't you just say so?"

She lifted her shoulder.

"It must be a challenge having a brother with special needs."

She shook her head. "I've never known anything different. Rory's great. He's smart as a whip. Plays chess. President of his high school computer club. He's pretty independent. He can walk with braces, but he also has really severe asthma. It's put him in the hospital more than once."

"He's sixteen?"

She smiled. "Almost seventeen, a fact that he feels compelled to regularly share with us."

"He's lucky to have you."

"I'm the lucky one. He gives me a hard time, knowing I'm working for you, but I know he loves me."

"Hard time?"

"Like I said. President of the computer club. A complete tech geek. His bedroom is a shrine to all things electronic."

His lips twitched. "Sounds like Wes."

"You're twins. Sure you aren't a tech geek, too?"

He laughed outright. "I'm business. Wes is development."

"And neither one of you were classified as geeks in the latest list of Austin's most eligible bachelors."

"Yeah, well, lists like that only look at marital status and bank balances." He jerked his chin toward the notebook. "They don't factor in fathers who lie about their identity and cheat on their wives."

"I think you're very eligible." The words came before she could stop them. "I've never met him, obviously, but your father can't be all bad. He founded Robinson Computers. I even know the company is active in philanthropic efforts because I read about them on the website. Those are good things."

He grunted. "You're better off not meeting my old man. But I'd like to meet Rory. President of the computer club? Impressive. That's something I never achieved."

She didn't believe he meant it, but she couldn't help appreciating the words. "He's also competing in a chess tournament next week at his school."

"What day?"

"Friday."

"All day?"

She nodded.

"Take the day off so you can be there."

"Thanks." She squeezed her armrest for a moment. "If you, um, if you really want to meet him, you could drop by the school."

Ben studied her face, looking for proof that she'd only made the invitation out of duty.

He found none.

He smiled slightly. "I'll check my schedule." Then, before he lost himself entirely in her eyes, he turned his attention back to her notes and cleared the strange constriction from his throat. "Keaton Whitfield. An architect, you say?"

"Yes." She sounded relieved to get the subject back on track. "Since he's in London, I wondered if you might find some help from the Fortunes themselves. Aren't some of them from England? That's only if we don't have luck reaching him directly, of course. I mean, you got hold of Randy, so maybe we'll have that sort of luck with Keaton."

He nodded, wondering why he hadn't thought of that himself. "But if we don't, the Fortune Chesterfields could be a place to start…"

* * *

"It was nice of Mr. Robinson to give you the day off," Ella's mother observed quietly for about the fifth time that day.

It was Friday. The day of Rory's chess tournament, and they were sitting on the bleachers in the gymnasium of Rory's school. The chess matches were set up on the floor at the far end of the gym and were down to the last two rounds. "It was." She propped her elbows on her knees, watching Rory study the board before making his move and hitting the time clock. "Rory looks tired. He's been using his inhaler a lot."

Elaine peered at her son. As the day had worn on, so had the onlookers—something not particularly encouraged at a chess tournament, anyway—but there were still a good fifty or so parents huddled in the section of seating allotted to them. "Yes, but he's determined. He'd never forgive me if I pulled him out at this point."

Ella knew that was true enough. She propped her elbows on her raised knees and cupped her chin on her hands.

"You look tired, too," Elaine murmured.

"I'm fine."

"Everything still going all right with your job?"

Ella had already told her mother all about the Boston trip the weekend before. Well, not *all* about the trip. But the sightseeing and the fancy hotel room and the food. "Fine. I haven't even seen B—Mr. Robinson since we got back, actually. He's been in California." A fact she'd learned from Mrs. Stone. Instead of leaving Ben written reports of her daily progress, she'd sent them to his personal email address. His responses had been brief to the point of terseness. Maybe because she'd had to tell him neither the Chicago nor Montreal leads had panned out, after all. Nor had she had any success getting Keaton Whitfield to respond to her messages.

"He travels a lot for Robinson Tech, it seems," Elaine said.

Someone sitting behind them shushed them.

Ella looked over her shoulder, mouthing *sorry*.

Ben had told her Henry lived with his parents now in California. Would he have tried to see the boy?

To see the boy's mother?

She didn't want to wonder. But she couldn't stop herself from doing so.

She suddenly stretched out her legs, unable to sit there and let her mind dwell on impossibilities. "I'm going to buy some lemonade," she whispered to her mom. "Do you want something?"

Elaine shook her head and patted her arm as Ella worked her way past her and down the tiered seats.

It had been nearly six years since Ella had walked the halls of the high school as a student, but nothing had changed. There were still vending machines located in the entryway of the gym, which did double duty as the school auditorium, and even though finding a drink had only been an excuse, she fed coins into the machine and waited for the bottle to drop.

It did.

But only partway, sticking halfway down.

"For crying out loud." She banged her palm against the glass front of the machine, trying to dislodge it.

"Got a problem there?"

She whirled around at the voice behind her and stared at Ben in shock. He was in one of his gray suits again, with a black-and-silver striped tie. She had the fanciful thought that he must own dozens of ties; she'd never seen the same one twice. "What are you doing here?"

His eyebrow peaked. "Did I mistake you inviting me last Saturday?"

"No! No, but I didn't even tell you what school."

He smiled faintly. "I have other means of discovering things than just you."

She flushed and his smile widened slightly.

"I wasn't sure you'd still be here," he added. "How's your brother doing?"

She felt strangely tongue-tied. "Very well. He's won all but two of his previous rounds, but he still has two more games to get through. And after six hours, I think he's looking pretty tired." Her brother was playing against some of the most talented kids in the state. None of whom had the physical challenges that Rory did. "He'll keep going, though. That's what Rory does."

"Good for him." He stepped closer and lifted his arm and she completely forgot how to breathe.

But all he did was smack the machine with a firm hand and her bottled lemonade tumbled down to the dispenser. "That's what you were banging on it for, right? Can't imagine you trying to get a bottle without paying for one."

She leaned over and retrieved the bottle from the bottom of the machine. "Yes. Would you like one?"

"Don't mind if I do," he said, surprising her into muteness again. He pulled several coins from his pocket and fed the machine. "My flight back was delayed and I haven't had a chance to eat."

She dared a glance at the vending machine next to the drink machine. It carried all manner of snacks from dried fruit to sweet rolls, but she couldn't imagine a single thing inside it appealing to Ben. "I think there are granola bars there."

His bottle—lemonade, just like hers—dropped without impedance and he plucked it from the dispensing tray. "Unless it's a rare steak, I'll pass. So." He looked toward the opened doorways on opposite ends of the entry. "Lead the way."

She hesitated. "My mother is here, too."

"Is that a problem for some reason?"

"Of course not." As long as her mother didn't make too big a deal out of Ella's boss showing up. She hadn't told Elaine that she'd mentioned the event to Ben.

He uncapped his bottle and took a long sip. "So, come on," he said when he lowered it again, and gestured with the bottle.

She honestly felt a need to gulp. She had never in a million years expected Ben to appear at the chess tournament. She also hadn't told Rory to expect him, since her brother would only be disappointed.

Yet here Ben was.

And suddenly it felt like sunshine wanted to burst out of her.

Chapter Eleven

"No *way*," Rory breathed, staring from the tablet computer Ben had just put in his hands to the man's face. "This is for *me*?"

"Unless you'd rather I give it to Janet Yee as consolation for the way you won the first-place trophy," he said drily.

He'd followed Ella and her mother and brother from the school to their home after the tournament, and from the corner of his eye, he could see the two women working in the kitchen while they prepared dinner.

Elaine's mother had insisted he join them, even though he'd have been happy to take them to any restaurant they chose. In celebration of Rory's spectacular win, he'd said. But mostly because it gave him a good excuse to close out a hellish week with at least the positive note that Ella always provided.

It was easy to see what she'd look like in another few decades. The only thing Ella hadn't inherited from her mother was her auburn hair. Elaine's hair was shoulder-length and brown without a hint of gray. But Ben figured he was probably as close to her age as he was to Ella's.

A helluva thought.

He looked back at Rory. The boy was taller than he'd expected, but he was every bit as sharp as Ella had claimed.

"It's time that Janet Yee had to share the spotlight," Elaine said, entering the living room. "The girl's been winning every tournament she enters for at least five years." She handed a thick white mug of coffee to Ben. "Cream or sugar?"

"This is perfect, thank you." He held up the mug in a toast to Rory. "So what's your next mountain to climb in the chess world?"

Rory's fingers were stroking the thin tablet, almost as if he was afraid to turn it on. "There's a regional tournament in a few months. But it's in San Francisco." He lifted his thin shoulder. "It'd mean hotels and stuff."

In other words, the cost of attending the tournament was an issue.

Ben gestured at the tablet. "Sell that," he suggested drily. "You've got it a full three months before we're releasing it."

"No *way*," Rory said again, clutching the tablet to his chest.

Elaine caught Ben's eye and they both chuckled.

"I was just in San Francisco on business," Ben told Rory. "Will the tournament there be held at a school, as well?"

Rory shook his head, naming some hotel. But Ben was having a hard time listening. In the kitchen, Ella had twisted her ponytail into a knot on top of her head and was bending over, pulling something from the oven. Her curvy, jean-clad rear made concentrating on her brother a challenge.

"Rory," Elaine interrupted. "Go and wash up for supper."

The teen looked ready to protest, but he set aside the

tablet and pulled himself to his feet with the aid of his metal crutches and left the room.

"It was very nice of you to come to the tournament," Elaine said when he was gone. "But the tablet is much too generous a gift."

"I'm not taking it back," he warned lightly. "Ask your daughter. She'll assure you I'm stubborn that way."

"He is," Ella said, coming in from the kitchen to set a casserole dish on the middle of the dining room table. "It's Mr. Robinson's way or the highway," she said lightly before hurrying back into the kitchen.

"My daughter says she had a lovely time in Boston. You arranged a private tour guide for her, I understand?"

He'd pawned off Ella on Johnny so he wouldn't be tempted to put his hands on her again. But he nodded, since—technically—Elaine's understanding wasn't incorrect.

"You're very generous."

"She was in Boston at my request. The least I could do was insure she had the chance to see some of the city while I was tied up with other business."

Elaine just smiled, but her eyes were definitely taking his measure.

So much so that he was a little relieved when Rory returned and started asking him a million questions about Robinson Tech that lasted all through their meal of some chicken concoction that was filling and unexpectedly tasty. Elaine followed that up with Rory's favorite dessert—angel food cake with peach sauce drizzled over it—and even though Ben figured it was well past time he excused himself, he couldn't make himself do it.

Instead, while Ella and Elaine were clearing the table again, he eyed Rory. "So, how about a chess game? You and me? It's been a while since I played, but—"

"I'll get the board," Rory interrupted, and shoved away

from the table so fast it was almost comical. He practically ran out of the room, his braces and legs so unevenly gaited that Ben got half out of his seat in case the kid fell.

Ella noticed. "Sit. He'll be fine. He doesn't appreciate too much assistance."

Ben sat back down and looked up at Ella as she retrieved the pad that had sat under the hot chicken dish. She was wearing a gray V-neck thermal shirt patterned with little orange flowers that clung to her curves, but it was the cluster of pale freckles on the back of her neck that taunted him most.

"I didn't know you played chess," she said.

"It's been a while."

Her eyes suddenly danced. "Hope you're prepared to lose, then."

He couldn't help smiling. "Maybe I won't lose. Want to place a wager?"

Ella laughed and shook her head. "No way, Mr. Robinson. I'm not naive enough to bet against you *or* my brother."

Before he could get too distracted by her, Rory came back with his chessboard and began setting up the pieces.

Ella returned to the kitchen, where her mom was still rinsing the dinner dishes at the sink.

"Go sit with them," Elaine urged softly when Ella began loading the dishwasher with the rinsed plates. "You obviously want to."

Ella avoided her mother's eyes. "He's just being nice."

"And what's wrong with a man who is nice?" Elaine turned off the faucet and handed the last plate to her. "Your father was a nice man, too."

Ella flushed and quickly shoved the plate into the dishwasher rack. "It's not like that."

"Isn't it?" Elaine leaned her hip against the counter, crossing her arms. "I see the way you look at him."

From the dining room table, Ella could hear Rory's adolescent voice and Ben's much deeper one as they trash-talked their way through their chess match.

The fact that Ben was making Rory laugh made her feel stupidly soft inside.

She dumped dishwashing powder in the dispenser and slammed the dishwasher door shut. "I don't know what you mean." She jabbed the button and started the noisy appliance, then reached for a dishtowel to wipe off her damp hands.

"Ella." Keeping her back toward the doorway leading to the living room, Elaine stepped into Ella's path, keeping her from escape. To further cement her position, she grabbed Ella's arm and pulled her into the laundry room, where their voices wouldn't travel. "You're a beautiful young woman and it's equally apparent to me that your Mr. Robinson is very aware of that fact."

"I don't need to be warned about getting in over my head, Mom. I know he's out of my league."

Elaine lifted her hand. "I wasn't finished."

Ella swallowed, looking at the ceiling.

"What I was going to say was that I also know how wide that streak of responsibility is that you possess," Elaine continued. "And I want to tell you to stop worrying so much about your brother and me. To stop worrying about your classes and medical bills and being the perfect daughter, which you are, anyway. Just be the beautiful young woman you are with a very nice man."

Ella looked at her mom. "What are you suggesting?"

Elaine laughed. "Good heavens, Ella, get that look off your face. I'm not suggesting you go out and seduce your boss. I'm just telling you to enjoy yourself for once. I'm not so doddering that I can't tell Mr. Robinson didn't come to dinner because he wanted my chicken casserole. He wanted more time with *you*. Not that you need to ask, but I'm telling you that I approve."

"It's *not* like that."

"You're not already halfway in love with him?"

Ella couldn't stand to hear anymore. Her face was already on fire. "Of course not. And he certainly doesn't feel like that about me. Why would he?"

Elaine smiled gently. "Honey, why *wouldn't* he?"

Ella shook her head vehemently. It was easier to deny now the very possibility that Ben was interested in anything more than sex from her—something in which he'd assured her he would never indulge—than to let herself hope for more later. "I'm not in the market for a broken heart," she told her mother, "and that's the end of it!"

She quickly left the laundry room and rushed out into the dining room, where Rory had already checkmated Ben.

Ben peeled out of his suitcoat. "Two out of three?" He glanced at Ella as he rolled up his shirtsleeves. "What's wrong?"

Her throat felt like a noose was tightening around it. "Nothing, if you don't count that spectacular loss." She gestured at the chessboard, where Rory had captured all but two of Ben's pieces. "How long ago did you say it was since you've played?"

Rory was cackling with laughter, obviously in his element as he reset the board. "I can spot you some pieces."

Ben gave him a mock glare. "You think, unless it's your king, I don't have a chance?"

Rory's shoulders bounced with his laughter. "Well—"

Ben finished rolling up his sleeves. "Get that chess clock I saw you had at the tournament."

Rory's eyebrows shot up his forehead.

"I'll get it," Ella said thickly and nearly jogged out of the room.

The clock—a new digital one that she'd bought Rory for Christmas—was sitting on his bed where he'd tossed it. Getting it had been only an excuse to gather her composure, which, with every passing moment, she was beginning to fear wasn't ever going to be possible.

Because Ella's mother was more right than she knew.

Ella wasn't halfway in love with Ben.

She was all the way, head over heels in love with him.

The second chess game was a draw.

The third, Ben managed to win. Though later, he wasn't really sure how.

"I hope your brother didn't *let* me win," he admitted to Ella when he finally made himself take his leave for the night.

They were standing on her front porch, the gold light of the plain light fixture shining weakly down on her head.

"Rory never lets anyone win," she assured him. She'd pulled on a sweater, but still had her arms crossed over her chest as if she was chilly. "He'll never forget this evening," she said. "It was, um, really nice of you to indulge him."

"I'm no more nice than I am generous."

Her eyes flew to his and he knew she was remembering that kiss just as well as he was. Then she looked away, moistening her lip and staring down at her shifting feet. "Fine. Thanks for selfishly spending the evening entertaining my brother. And for the tablet. But you really didn't need to give him anything." She scuffed her shoe against the cement porch. "We're not charity cases."

He went still. "Is that what you think?"

She looked up then, looking so miserable he was damnably afraid he could see a sign of tears in her eyes. "What were you really doing here, Ben?"

Hollowness suddenly opened up inside his chest. "It can't just be celebrating a kid's chess win?"

She moistened her lips again. And there was definitely a visible sheen to her full lips. "I don't think so."

He shoved his hands into his suit pockets to keep from touching her. "I had a bitch of a week," he said abruptly.

"You were in California. Mrs. Stone told me." She scuffed her foot again. "Did you see…see Henry?"

He frowned, genuinely shocked. "Henry! I told you he's gone."

"He's in California."

"San Diego. I was in San Francisco trying and mostly failing to pull a business deal out of the fire. The cities aren't exactly on the same block." He peered at her face. "Pursuing Henry is pointless. I have no legal standing. No biological tie." His voice went gruff. "Just memories of a little kid I never wanted to want in the first place getting under my skin."

The knot she'd pulled her hair into had loosened and she tucked a lock behind her ear. "What about your old girlfriend? His mother?"

"Stephanie? If I'd have had a way of saving him from her, I would have."

She angled her head at that, frowning at him. "What's that mean?"

"That he's saddled with a money-hungry bitch for a mom?"

"If she was money hungry, why'd she ever let *you* know he wasn't yours?"

"This is the last thing I expected to get into tonight."

"Okay, so what did you expect?"

"I needed a break!" His voice started to rise and he exhaled. "I told you that it's been a bad week."

She tightened her arms around her chest. "I'm sorry. It's none of my business."

He shoved his fingers through his hair and stared over her shoulder at the house next to the Thomases. It was the

mirror opposite of Ella's, with a waist-high hedge separating the driveways.

The modest, aging homes were poles away from the lavish estate where he'd grown up. And he tried to remember
times spent in his own home where he'd felt as easy and
as...calm...as he had tonight, and he couldn't.

"First off, I don't do girlfriends. Ever. But for about
three months, Stephanie Blakely and I were lovers because
it suited us both. She wanted money and made no bones
about it. She liked being on my arm, and I liked knowing
I'd never fall in love with her. Sorry if that sounds calculated, but I've already warned you I'm not a nice guy."

"You don't have to tell me any of—"

He cut her off. "When the Robinson luster wore off—
and it always does, regardless of the dollar signs—she
moved on. No harm, no foul. She came back with Henry
when he was a year old, telling me he was mine." His jaw
tightened. "I told you already, the timing was right. The
blood types were right. It made sense and I let myself believe her. I said I'd take care of them. I moved her into
my house. I even started to care about Henry. Then ten
months later, Henry's real father showed up, DNA tests in
hand. But I didn't give up that easily. I had my own DNA
test done. And it proved what blood types didn't. Henry
wasn't mine." His hands curled into fists as he forced himself to finish the story. "For all of Stephanie's interest in
my money, and I offered her a lot to stay—"

The shock filling her eyes was visible even in the thin
porch light.

"—she still took Henry and went back to California,"
he said flatly. "End of story. No happily-ever-afters. Not
with them."

Annoyed because his voice sounded hoarse and his
chest ached, he stepped down the porch ramp, intent on
leaving.

But the second he did, Ella said his name and he stopped.

Then she leaned forward and wrapped her arms around his neck. With the advantage of the ramp added to her height, her eyes were almost on a level with his. "I'm sorry," she whispered and hugged him.

Before he even had a chance to register her pressed against him, she was pulling back again. "If you need a reason, just blame that on being nice to my brother. Because you were, whether you want to admit it or not." She edged closer to the house door. "And I'll report to work on Monday like usual. If you've decided I'm not the right person to help—"

"Shut up."

Her full lips pressed together.

"Monday," he said. "I have another person to add to your plate."

"Another woman of your father's?"

"In a matter of speaking. His mother. His real mother, Jacqueline Fortune, not the made-up fiction he gave us our whole lives. Only I can't find a straight answer on whether she's alive or not. Maybe you'll have better luck."

"Okay."

He took several steps down the driveway toward his Porsche, which stuck out like a sore thumb parked at the curb in front of the house. Then he looked back at her. "Tell your mother thank you again for including me this evening. I don't remember a dinner that I've enjoyed as much."

"I will."

He drove away with the sight of Ella still standing on the porch, the light shining on her hair.

He'd never wanted to leave somewhere less in his life.

Ella locked her bicycle up outside Ben's house again on Monday morning and once again used her key to go inside when Mrs. Stone failed to answer the buzzer. Even though Ben had never asked her to work over the weekends, she'd come to work that morning armed with more information she'd gathered over the weekend about the Fortune family. There was a lot of information to be garnered over the internet about Ben's family, but there was even more about the Fortunes.

Not only was there Kate Fortune and her world-famous cosmetics, but there were also Fortunes in California and Georgia and here in Texas, as well as Lady Josephine Fortune Chesterfield's assorted British offspring.

Since she knew Keaton Whitfield was located in London, she started with one of Lady Josephine's sons, Charles, who also lived there and held a position with the British tourism department. But trying to reach him through his work when she'd called earlier that morning from home had proved as fruitless as her efforts to reach Keaton Whitfield directly. Not that that was much of a surprise to Ella. If she were ever hounded by the paparazzi the way Charles was, she wouldn't take calls from absolute strangers, either.

It was the paparazzi reports, though, that gave Ella her next idea, since it was the gossip websites that led her to Charles's sister, Lucie, who'd been reportedly seen traveling to Texas to visit her sister, Amelia.

The question remaining was whether Lucie was still *in* Texas.

Ella made her way up the stairs to Ben's office without encountering Mrs. Stone and her focus strayed to the closed door of Henry's bedroom. Sighing a little, she went into the office and dumped her bag on the floor behind the desk before sitting down at the computer.

Ben had left another neatly typed note for her with the information he had about Jacqueline Fortune. Once again, Ella couldn't help feeling warmed by the fact that he wanted her help on that search, as well.

He'd scrawled a handwritten *thanks* at the bottom of the page and she placed her hand over it for a moment before sliding the sheet to the side and opening up her notebook, where she'd made her notes over the weekend.

She pulled out the computer keyboard and began quickly pecking at the keys. All she had to do was type in *Lucie Chesterfield* and a slew of mentions appeared on the screen. Mostly they were in conjunction with her sister, Amelia, who'd caused a terrific scandal a few years before when she'd supposedly dumped an English viscount in favor of a no-name rancher from Horseback Hollow.

A Texan would have had to have been living under a rock to miss the furor that had caused. Ella remembered it well, because Rory had been in the hospital with a respiratory infection at the time and she'd spent hours in his hospital room while the television news dwelled on the scandal.

As Ella trolled the internet, she thought the photographs that she found of Amelia and her "Horseback Hollow Home Wrecker"—the term bestowed on the rancher Quinn Drummond—showed a handsome couple obviously devoted to each other. They'd even married and had a doll of a baby girl.

Amelia and her royal connections obviously hadn't put *her* too far out of the small-town rancher's league.

Pushing aside the thought, Ella focused her attention more closely on figuring out a way to reach Lucie. She remembered very well from Kate Fortune's party the hostess's mention of the Fortune Foundation, and there was a new branch of the agency located in Horseback Hollow. It wasn't such a stretch to imagine that Lucie might have some involvement with the foundation, considering her own charitable activities, which were copiously chronicled.

Short of that, Ella supposed just showing up in the small town and yelling their names might garner some response.

Shaking her head at her own silliness, she pulled up the website for the foundation and tracked down the staff listing. She hadn't really expected to find Lucie on it, but she called the Horseback Hollow office, anyway.

The girl who answered the phone was obviously young. "I'm sorry, ma'am," she said in response to Ella's request to speak to the office manager, "but everyone's in a meeting right now for our fund-raising event tomorrow. Can I leave a message?"

Ella idly clicked through the links on the computer, bringing up images of Fortunes located far and wide. "Where's the event again?"

"The elementary school," the other girl answered as if it should have been obvious. "They're giving out books to all of the third and fourth graders—"

"Oh, right." Horseback Hollow was a tiny town. Maybe not as tiny since as the theme park, Cowboy Country, had opened up there a year ago, but still, it was barely a dot on the map in comparison to Austin. How many elementary schools could the town possess?

"If you're with the media, they'll be offering statements in the school cafeteria after the book distribution. About ten a.m."

"They?"

The girl sighed again, as if all this information should have been obvious. "Christopher Fortune, of course. He runs this location."

"Will anyone else be there?"

"Oh, I suppose you mean his cousin? Lady Amelia— well, she's Mrs. Drummond now, but everyone still keeps calling her that—is supposed to be there. And her sister—"

Ella held her breath.

"—Lucie will be there, too, but neither one of them are scheduled to speak, so—"

"Thanks," Ella interrupted. "You've been very helpful."

"If you want to make a donation to the foundation, you can visit our website at www-dot—"

"Got it!" Ella quickly hung up, feeling only a little guilty.

She found the calendar of events on the Fortune Foundation's Horseback Hollow website and sure enough, the book giveaway was listed.

She opened up the phone app and called Ben, too excited to wait. As he'd assured her, when she gave her name to his secretary, Bonita immediately connected her with his office.

"Ella? What's wrong?"

Her stomach squiggled around at the sound of his deep voice coming out of the speakers and filling the room. "Nothing. I'm sorry to bother you at work—"

"You're not bothering me. Hold on a sec." She heard him speaking to someone else, then a moment later, he was back. "Had someone in my office," he said. "What's up?"

"I have a line on Lucie Fortune Chesterfield's whereabouts," she said quickly. "Remember she's one of the Fortunes who lives in—"

"London."

For some reason, she typed in a search for "Ben Robinson office" and up popped an image from a technical magazine with him on the cover. Maybe it was a studio shot. Or maybe that was actually his desk he was leaning against.

"And?" he prompted.

She recentered her thoughts. "London. Right. Anyway, she's in Texas right now...oh. I wonder if she was at Kate Fortune's party? I don't remember seeing her."

"Ella—"

"Right!" She nervously rose from his chair and moved around behind it, squeezing her hands over the back. "She's going to be at an event at an elementary school in Horseback Hollow tomorrow morning. Would you be able to get away to meet with her? See if you can enlist her help in meeting Keaton Whitfield?"

He muttered a soft oath. "I'm speaking at a thing tomorrow at the university."

"Of Texas?" She immediately resumed her seat and started typing again.

He laughed softly and her fingers curled against the keyboard. "Yes. The University of Texas."

"What sort of thing?"

"A symposium of business leaders."

"I found it."

"Found what?"

She flushed, looking away from the computer screen, where she'd pulled up a graphic of the symposium schedule. On it, Ben was clearly listed as the keynote speaker. "You're kind of a big deal, aren't you?"

He laughed softly again and Ella closed her eyes, savoring the sound.

"You can go to Horseback Hollow and talk to Lucie yourself," he suggested. "I'll arrange a charter flight tomorrow morning. You could be there in a little over an hour. Talk to her and get back to town by tomorrow night."

"Without you?"

"I trust you."

Ella exhaled carefully.

"Okay," she said faintly.

As if she had any other choice when Ben asked something of her.

Chapter Twelve

She flew out of the same executive airport that they'd used going to Boston.

Her blue suit was getting a workout. She'd worn it more in the past two and a half weeks than she had in the two years since she'd bought it at a department-store clearance sale.

The novelty of the flight was nowhere near as interesting as it had been with Ben's company, and she spent the eighty-minute flight immersed in her Intro to Taxation book, since the class started that week. Unfortunately, the subject was considerably less interesting than remembering in vivid detail the last time she'd flown with Ben.

When the plane landed, she figured she'd be lucky if she remembered even a third of what she'd actually read.

Miraculously, there was a car waiting for her at the small airstrip, driven by one of the Fortune Foundation representatives.

"We're so pleased that Robinson Tech is taking an interest in the foundation," the young man said, greeting her with an enthusiastic pump of her hand. "I can't tell you what the donation they've promised will mean."

Once again, Ben was doing things not exactly according to plan. He'd said nothing about making a donation to the foundation. She was becoming less surprised by the day.

The man who proclaimed his selfishness was proving to be anything but.

It took no time at all to drive to the elementary school, where a few local news outlets were set up in the cafeteria.

"They're still doing the book distribution if you want a peek," her escort offered.

She nodded eagerly, far more interested in seeing that than hanging around in the cafeteria with reporters. "Thank you."

The children's books—dozens and dozens—were stacked on long tables in the gym, surrounded by excited kids. In one corner, Amelia Drummond sat on the floor with a darling petite infant girl on her lap, reading from a picture book to the kids circled around her. In another corner, a tall, good-looking man was grinning as he held a book out of reach from a little boy who was bouncing up and down on his feet, trying to catch it.

And in yet another corner, filling fabric bags with books that she passed out to each child in a line, Ella spotted Lucie Fortune Chesterfield.

She immediately felt like the country mouse faced with the city mouse. Lucie was taller and thinner than Ella, and positively exuded elegance and grace.

She also had a surprisingly kind smile when Ella approached her once the line of children had finished.

"Hello." She extended her long, slender hand. "I'm Lucie. Do you have a child here at the school?"

Ella quickly shook her head. Lucie's hand was cool and smooth. "I don't have any children."

Lucie's smile widened and she tucked her long brown hair behind her ear. "I thought you looked a bit young." She had a very distinct English accent that struck Ella as extremely proper. "Are you a teacher?"

"No, actually, I'm from Austin. My name's Ella Thomas." She didn't figure she had much time, whether or not Ben had promised an exorbitant donation to the Fortune Foundation. "Benjamin Robinson sent me to speak with you."

Lucie's hazel gaze sharpened. "Ben Robinson," she repeated. "From Robinson Tech."

"Yes, he—"

"Made quite a splash at a party I attended recently with my mother and sister." Lucie studied her. "You were there, weren't you?" she said slowly. "With the catering staff?"

Ella hadn't remembered seeing Lucie at Kate Fortune's party. But then there'd been quite a crowd, and once she'd served Ben his Manhattan, she hadn't been aware of much of anything else. "Yes." She was afraid the other woman might have some comment about Ella going from being on a catering crew to acting as Ben's personal emissary, but then realized that Lucie was far too gracious to do any such thing. "I know this is out of left field, approaching you like this, but if I could have just a few private minutes—"

"Of course." Lucie came around the table and gestured for Ella to follow her. She stopped only briefly to buss the moppet sitting on her sister's lap with a kiss, then they finished crossing the gymnasium. "My niece, Clementine. I'm absolutely in love with her. Haven't been able to make myself go back to London yet." They entered one of the empty classrooms next door, where Lucie closed the door. "So, what can I do for you, Ms. Thomas?"

"Ella, please."

"Lovely name." Lucie perched on a corner of the teacher's cluttered desk. "Wonderfully old-fashioned." Her tone was friendly. Confiding. Almost as if they were two girlfriends who'd gotten together for a chat. "So, do you think he's really a Fortune? Your Benjamin?"

Ella couldn't call Ben hers no matter how much she wished she could. "Yes, I do."

"Which makes him a cousin of some sort to me." Lucie crossed her ankles. "And family does for family." She raised her eyebrows slightly.

"Ben would like to meet Keaton Whitfield," Ella said, taking her cue. "He's an architect based in London."

"If he wants an architect, surely he could hire the man straight out?"

Ella hesitated for a moment. Aside from saying he trusted her, he hadn't given her any other guidance about his situation when it came to dealing with Lucie. "He doesn't want to hire him," she admitted. Then just went with her gut. "Mr. Whitfield may be a Fortune, as well."

Lucie's eyebrows inched up a little higher. "Why would your Benjamin think that?"

"Because there's a possibility they could be brothers."

"Oh, my." Lucie uncrossed her ankles and sat forward a little. "So he could also be a cousin of sorts to me, as well."

Ella nodded.

"What's your interest in all of this?"

"I'm just working for Ben."

Lucie's eyes were kind. But they were assessing, nonetheless. "Is that all?"

Ella started to deny it. There was no reason for her to admit anything, but there was just something about Lucie. "No," she admitted, and it was a relief to finally say it aloud. "But that's all on me. He's Ben Robinson, for goodness' sake. I'm—" she twitched her blue skirt "—exactly what I look like. A typical college student who works temp jobs at parties that people like you and him attend as guests."

Lucie made a face. "I'd hardly say typical. That *Ben*

Robinson—" she ran the name together in the same way Ella had "—sent you here, after all, on what's obviously a sensitive personal matter." She looked away and for a moment, her hazel eyes seemed lost in memory. "And the heart wants what it wants."

Ella flushed, not at all comfortable with being so transparent.

Then Lucie looked back at her and smiled. "Don't give up, Ella."

"On reaching Keaton Whitfield?"

"That, too." Lucie's eyes suddenly twinkled. "I'll see what I can do to smooth the path between your Benjamin and this architect. He's based in London, you say?"

"Yes." Ella handed over one of Ben's business cards. "If you have any luck at all, you can reach us at any one of those numbers." She'd also written down both her and Ben's email addresses.

Lucie tucked the card in the pocket of her perfectly tasteful red dress and they left the classroom again.

The moment she showed her face in the gymnasium, she was hailed and shuffled off along with her sister, presumably to the cafeteria to pose for the press.

Ella could have hung around, but she'd gotten more than what she'd come for.

She found the guy who'd picked her up still waiting outside the school and he drove her back to the airstrip.

Less than a half hour later, she was again in the air and it was still afternoon when she landed again in Austin, where the same driver who'd transported her to the airport took her back home again. Knowing that Ben would still be tied up with the symposium, she called his office and left a message with his secretary, figuring he'd be in touch with Bonita no matter how busy he was.

On that score, she was correct.

Ben called her within a half hour and she relayed the results of her meeting.

"Good work."

"Thanks." She felt strangely tongue-tied. "How's the symposium going?"

"Dry, dry and more dry."

"Ah. It's an *accounting* symposium?"

He laughed. "Bonita's going to email you some documents for you to sign," he said. "Watch for them."

"What sort of documents?"

"Passport application."

Ella's breath left her chest.

"Ella?"

"I'm here," she managed to respond. "We already talked about this."

"Yeah, but I'm not the sort who gives up after the first no. If Lucie gets us an in with Whitfield, I want to be prepared."

"It takes weeks to get a passport, doesn't it?"

"Not if you have the right connections. And the governor is one of mine."

"Right," she said faintly. Then she swallowed and cleared her throat. "Whether you get me a passport or not doesn't mean I'm going to go to London with you."

"You'll be safe," he said smoothly. "Nothing will happen like before."

What if I don't want to be safe?

She wanted to blurt out the words.

But of course, she didn't.

"You don't need me to go with you."

"Just sign the forms," he said again.

"You're looking very wide-eyed, Ella Thomas."

"Am I?" She stared at Ben, hardly believing that they were aboard a jetliner that would deposit them at London

Heathrow Airport. Their first-class seats weren't next to each other, but were situated one in front of the other, angled in toward the windows. There was even a flat-screen television in each seat's area. "The seat goes all the way flat into a bed," she said, not caring whether she sounded as wide-eyed as she looked or not.

His lips tilted. For only the second time since she'd met him, he wasn't wearing a suit, but an untucked black T-shirt over dark blue jeans. He looked younger and even more handsome, if that was possible. "Makes nearly ten hours of flying time a little more bearable," he assured her. "You're going to want to sleep. It'll be just after nine in the morning when we land."

She pressed her palm nervously to her belly. "Sure you couldn't have just talked to Keaton Whitfield on the phone?" She knew the unlikelihood of that even when she said the words, but she couldn't help it. Everything about the last few days had been more surreal than ever.

She had a newly minted passport in her messenger bag, procured in what she was certain had been a record amount of time, since it hadn't even been a week since she'd met with Lucie Fortune Chesterfield. To say the other woman had come through for them was an understatement. She'd contacted Ben that very same day to say she'd paved the way for a meeting with the architect. All Ben had to do was say when he could get to London.

"You could have already been there to meet with Keaton by now," Ella pointed out, not for the first time. She glanced past Ben to where the flight attendants were busily settling the last few passengers into the first-class cabin. "Instead of waiting for my passport to come through."

"Consider it another history lesson in your travel arsenal. We've seen Boston. Now you can see England."

She rolled her eyes, laughing a bit despite herself. "I

don't need a first-class ticket to London as a refresher course on the Revolutionary War."

"Yeah, well, it never hurts the governor to know Robinson Tech owes him one."

She flushed, just thinking about it.

"Mr. Robinson, if you'll take your seat, we're readying for takeoff."

Ben glanced at the flight attendant and nodded, then looked back at Ella. "Put on your earphones, order some wine when they ask and relax," he advised."

She gave him a look. "I can do that a lot easier than you can," she challenged. "You probably won't even put away your cell phone until we're over the ocean."

He laughed and showed the cell phone in question tucked in the palm of his long-fingered hand. Then he flipped the device into her lap. "Guard it yourself, then."

She caught the phone before it slid off her lap onto the floor. Before she could hand it back to him, he'd moved around to take his own seat, and she leaned her head back against her wide plush headrest, hauling in a deep breath.

Maybe it was a good thing she couldn't really see him well from here, she decided.

The flight attendant was moving through the cabin, giving her safety spiel, from which, evidently, even first-class passengers weren't exempt. Ella listened with half an ear while she ran her thumb across the front of Ben's fancy phone.

The second she did, the screen lit up.

The flight attendant stopped next to Ella. "You'll need to turn that off now, I'm afraid, Ms. Thomas," she said with a smile, before moving on again.

The directive helped alleviate the intense curiosity seizing Ella, considering the phone was practically an extension of Ben himself.

She quickly leaned forward and held out the phone between her fingers to reach around the side of Ben's seat. "I don't know how to turn it off."

His hand brushed hers, seeming to linger as he took the phone back from her.

She curled her fingers against her palm and quickly sat back again, dragging the guidebook to London she'd borrowed from the library out of the cubby drawer where she'd stuffed it before fastening her seat belt.

She wished she could blame her racing heartbeat on the increasing thrum of the jet engines as the plane moved away from the airport terminal. But it would be pointless.

Instead, she looked out one of the two windows beside her seat, watching the deepening sunset of the sky outside and wondering what she'd done in her life to end up here at this moment, flying partway around the world with a man she could love for the rest of her life. If only he'd let her.

It was raining when they landed.

Even though Ella had slept for a few hours on the plane, her nerves had kept her from relaxing entirely. Ben, on the other hand, looked as clear-eyed as he always did. The only change for him was the decidedly sexy shadow of dark whiskers softening his sharp jaw. A shadow he'd shaved off before they even left the plane, much to her chagrin.

She wondered just how shocked he'd be if she told him how much she liked the look on him.

They joined the line at border control, where she presented her stiffly new passport for the first time ever. In the next line over, from the corner of her eye, she saw Ben pass over his passport, considerably more well-used than hers. Then they were through and off to collect their luggage. There wasn't much, since they weren't planning to stay but a couple of days. Ben simply had the same garment bag he'd used when they'd gone to Boston.

Ella had upgraded to an inexpensive rolling bag that her

mother had insisted on purchasing for her. Ella suspected the gift was as much to make certain that Ella didn't back out at the last second and refuse to go to London altogether.

She wasn't surprised to find that there was a driver waiting for them, holding a neatly printed placard with *Robinson* on it.

"Thank Bonita," he told her when they were in the car driving away from the airport and she asked if he had drivers waiting on call for him all over the world. "She arranges all this stuff for me."

"Did she arrange Johnny for you, too?"

"She scheduled him." He'd powered up his cell phone the moment they'd landed and he had it in his hand now. "Do you want to call your mother?"

It was six hours earlier in Austin. "She'd still be at work."

He nudged the phone into her hand. "Call her, then. Let her know you're here safe and sound."

Ella's mother hadn't seemed worried about Ella traveling with Ben. It was only *Ella* who was doing that. "Won't it cost you a fortune on your cell phone bill if I call Texas?"

He gave her a dry look. "Haven't we established my feelings on the issue of cost?"

Much too aware of the press of his thigh against hers in the back of the car—which was much smaller than anything they'd ridden in together before—she dialed her mother at work. Once Elaine answered, Ella didn't linger over talking. She was too conscious of Ben hearing every word. She promised to check in again if she had the chance, then held out the phone to Ben again. "Thank you."

"Anytime." He pocketed the phone and looked out the side window at the congested traffic. "We're not meeting Whitfield until tonight for drinks. That leaves plenty of time if you want to stop and say howdy to the Queen."

Ella laughed, as he'd obviously meant her to. "What

have you told Keaton? Did you take a similar tack with him as you did Randy?"

He shook his head. The only indication she had that he wasn't entirely as blasé as he appeared was the rhythmic thump of his thumb against the seat between them. "I could tell a more straightforward approach was necessary. I told him I had a personal matter I wanted to discuss. Thanks to Lucie greasing the wheels, he agreed."

She was suddenly worried all over again. "You don't think Lucie told him anything more, do you?"

He shook his head and Ella relaxed again.

Then Ben looked out the window again, not seeming to want to talk, and so she did the same.

They arrived at the hotel and even though it was early, they were still checked in. Ella had thought her room in Boston was spectacular. Here, though, her room was actually more of a suite that was even more luxurious. And when she looked out the windows, she saw a park that looked glorious even on a drizzling January day. She could only imagine what Ben's room was like.

But then again, she *could* imagine. And that was one of the reasons why her nerves felt nearly shredded.

He'd told her to relax for an hour or so, and then they'd meet in the lobby and decide where to go from there.

Even though the bed looked inviting, she knew better than to lie down and take the snooze she was suddenly almost desperate to have. Instead, she went into the bathroom that was completely outfitted in Carrara marble, from the oval-shaped bathtub to the separate shower, the floors and even the walls. She stripped out of her jeans and sweater, leaving them in a heap on the floor along with her bra and panties, and turned on the shower. Soon, steam was filling the spacious room, and she stepped under the spray, lathering up with the luscious gels and shampoos provided for her.

After, wrapped in one of the thick white robes the hotel provided, she finally turned to open her suitcase. Even though Ben had told her when they checked in that someone would unpack her suitcase for her, she couldn't imagine leaving it for a hotel person to do.

Her blue suit was packed neatly inside, and she pulled it out, feeling herself go pale when she saw the bleached-white splotch on the very front of the skirt after she pulled off the cleaner's plastic.

She'd picked the suit up from the cleaner's the afternoon before and stuck it straight into her suitcase. Never in her life had she imagined the cleaners might have damaged it.

She sank down on the ivory duvet that covered the wide bed. She hadn't brought a backup, either. All she had inside her suitcase were her underclothes, an extra pair of jeans and a few warm shirts.

What on earth was she going to wear when they met Keaton Whitfield later that evening? She knew the restaurant where they were going wasn't a place she could just show up at wearing faded blue jeans.

Hating that she felt close to tears, she transferred the rest of her clothes to the closet, leaving out only fresh undies, and stuck the suitcase on the high shelf before closing the door.

She thought she was imagining it when she heard a knock on her door. But when it was repeated, she cleared her throat and tightened the belt of the robe as she walked over to the door. She stood on her tiptoes to look through the peephole and saw Ben standing on the other side.

Without thinking, she unlocked the door and pulled it open. "What's wrong?"

His gaze ran over her and even though she was covered from neck nearly to toes in thick white terry cloth, she felt herself flush.

"Your hair is wet."

Her hand flew to her head. She probably still looked like a drowned rat. "I showered," she said inanely.

"I'll come back." He turned away.

"No, wait." Again, acting purely on instinct, she reached out and grabbed his arm. Just as quickly, when she became conscious of what she was doing, she released him again. "I thought you said we'd meet in the lobby."

He looked at her, seeming pained. "I did. Then—" He sighed. "Hell."

"Ben? What is it?"

"I got too keyed up to hang around in my suite," he admitted. "I didn't realize you'd be—" He gestured, not finishing.

"I was just going to dry my hair." She chewed the inside of her cheek. "You could wait here if you wanted. It won't take me long."

"That's not a good idea, Ella."

"Why? There's plenty of room in my suite."

His lips twisted. "I know you're not that naive."

Heat swept through her. Not of the embarrassment variety, either.

She tugged the belt tighter again, trying not to wonder what he'd do if she pulled it off instead and presented herself to him as naked as she'd been born. "Fine." Her voice sounded as tight as the belt. "I'll meet you in the lobby in a little bit, like we said."

His jaw canted to one side. "It's better that way," he said in a low voice.

Ella nodded, not speaking. He stepped back enough for her to shut the door, and she pushed it closed, flipping the lock.

Shuddering, she leaned back against the door and drew in a long, deep breath. Only in another country for a few hours and she was already in danger of throwing herself at him.

Surely she had more control than that? Then she laughed hollowly, because she didn't have more control.

Given the slightest hint from him, she'd throw herself into his arms and she knew it. Sighing, she pushed away from the door and went to dry her hair.

Less than ten minutes later, she was dressed again and she went down to find him in the lobby. Not surprisingly, she caught him talking on his cell phone, though he ended the call as soon as he spotted her.

"I need to find a shop," she said abruptly.

"What do you need?"

She told him about her ruined skirt. "Unless you'll change your mind about meeting Keaton on your own, I'll need something a little more presentable than jeans to wear."

He looked like he was considering debating the point.

"I did an internet search on the place where he's meeting us," she said. "It's not a jeans sort of establishment."

"Always prepared, aren't you?"

"I try to be." Her smile felt tight. "Except I didn't think to bring a backup outfit for tonight."

"Shopping it is."

"Somewhere inexpensive," she warned as they headed toward the hotel entrance. "We both know I don't have a fortune to spend."

He smiled suddenly, and settled his palm on the small of her back. "Ella, sweetheart. I *do*."

Chapter Thirteen

Six hours later, Ella's mouth was no longer dry because she was simply dazed.

Not only had Ben insisted on taking her to Harrods, where her eyes had popped out from sticker shock, but he'd also insisted on purchasing whatever she needed.

Her version of what she'd needed varied dramatically from his, though, and instead of leaving the store with a quickly purchased skirt that she could wear that evening, he'd escorted her through the expensive department store, carelessly assuring her that the few outfits he chose for her to try on were more in the nature of a uniform.

She'd looked at him as if he'd gone crazy.

But neither had she absolutely refused him, either.

Perhaps it was because when she'd modeled the leather Alexander McQueen cropped jacket and coordinating pencil skirt for him, he'd stopped looking at his cell phone every five minutes. And when she'd twirled around in front of him wearing a black-and-blue mini sheath dress that fit her like a glove, he'd smiled and swirled his finger in the air and she'd twirled all over again.

Eventually, though, the demands of his cell phone had intruded, because even though she was feeling like Cinderella in a fairy tale, he was still the COO of Robinson Tech and that responsibility followed him 24/7.

He'd passed her into the hands of a very capable personal shopper and returned to the hotel to take care of his business.

He hadn't returned. But Ella hadn't minded all that much. She'd spent the rest of the afternoon in hedonistic pleasure in the salon where her freshly washed hair had been washed all over again, trimmed and then coaxed into artfully natural waves; her hands had been manicured and her feet pedicured. When she'd finally left the department store, she felt glossy from head to toe, and beneath the swinging cashmere coat that Ben had chosen for her before he'd left, she was wearing the pretty sheath dress and unfamiliarly high black heels.

The personal shopper had promised to have her original clothing and the rest of her purchases delivered to the hotel.

And now, Ella stood on the street outside the restaurant where she and Ben were to meet Keaton Whitfield. She started to check the watch on her wrist before remembering that for the first time in forever, she wasn't wearing it. She'd left it with the rest of her things, packaged up to be transported to the hotel. She still figured she was a few minutes early. But it was drizzling, and she had even less desire to stand out in the rain and let the hairdresser's efforts go to waste than she did to enter the restaurant without Ben. So she went inside.

Even on a Monday evening, the restaurant was clearly busy. She surrendered her coat to the coat check and when she gave Ben's name, the maître d' immediately escorted her to a table on the far side of the room, and she smiled to herself at the sight of Ben already there, sitting facing away from the door in a high-backed booth.

She stopped next to him. "Well, I hope the bill that you're going to get is worth it," she said. "I've been buffed from head—" She broke off when the man turned and looked at her, and she realized it wasn't Ben at all.

Just a man that looked stunningly similar to him.

If for no other reason, she pegged him at that very moment as Ben's brother.

"Mr. Whitfield?"

He rose from the booth and smiled at her. "Yes."

She stuck out her hand. "Ella Thomas. I'm a—"

"Associate of Ben Robinson's," he said, shaking her hand slowly. "He told me." His eyes roved over her in an eerily familiar way. "He neglected to warn me how lovely you were."

Ella tugged her hand away, flushing a little. The man was attractive, to be sure. But he wasn't Ben. "Thank you."

"Please. Have a seat." Keaton gestured at the bench opposite the one he'd occupied.

Coming into the restaurant, Ben had a strong sense of déjà vu when he saw Ella across the room, sliding into the booth, displaying a hell of a lot of creamy, shapely leg as she did so.

The fact that the man standing beside the booth was also appreciating the display didn't escape him, either.

He'd already realized that dealing with Whitfield was going to be an entirely different game than it had been with Randy Phillips. But seeing the man looking at *his* Ella made something inside him fill with fury.

He strode across the room and Ella turned toward him.

Her face broke into a smile at the sight of him, her eyes almost seeming to sparkle, and the fury inside him stuttered.

He almost had it under control by the time he reached

the table and Ella slid over to make room for him to sit beside her.

"Ben," she said, gesturing to the man still standing there. "This is Keaton Whitfield. Mr. Whitfield, my, uh—" She stumbled for just a moment. "Ben Robinson," she said.

Ben dragged his unwilling eyes from her beautiful face to the man they'd come across the pond to see.

Keaton was eyeing him just as narrowly as Ben realized he was doing. They shook hands briefly, then just stood there looking at each other.

Ella laughed lightly, obviously hoping to lighten the moment. "Perhaps sitting might be an idea?"

Keaton relaxed first, his lips twisting wryly. He took the bench opposite Ella, and Ben sat down beside her, way too aware of the warmth of her only inches away.

Keaton gestured for one of the waiters. "Maybe a drink would serve us well."

Ben heartily agreed. He repeated Keaton's order for whiskey, neat, and Ella ordered wine.

When the waiter departed again, they just sat there looking at each other.

Once again, Keaton broke first. "It's probably going to be obvious when I say you look oddly familiar."

Ben didn't even realize he'd reached for Ella's hand until he felt the start she gave. He quickly let go again. "Might as well get to it," he said as he pulled out his wallet and extracted the small photograph he had of his father that had been taken many years earlier. "Do you know him?"

Keaton took the snapshot, his eyebrows yanking together over his long nose. "Where'd you get this?"

"It's my father," Ben said. "Gerald Robinson. Maybe you'd know him as Jerome Fortune, though. He founded Robinson Computers."

Keaton set the photograph carefully on the table, pulling

his hand away as if he didn't want to touch it any longer. "Thought the company was changing its name."

"It has," Ella answered when Ben didn't. He felt the weight of her gaze but couldn't look away from the other man. "It's Robinson Tech now," she explained.

"Do you recognize him?" Ben asked again.

Keaton nodded. "Only from one photograph to another. I don't know his name. Never did. But I'm pretty sure he's the bastard who broke my mother's heart after he left her pregnant." He met Ben's eyes. "With me."

Silence descended on the table again, broken only by the waiter, who returned with their drinks.

When Ben felt Ella's hand squeeze his, he exhaled. Everything he'd suspected had coalesced in the form of the man—his half brother—who sat across from them.

"I'm sorry," he said quietly. "I'm afraid my father has probably broken a lot of hearts along the way."

Keaton studied him for a long moment. "Why are you here? What do you want?"

"To find out if there are more children of Gerald Robinson."

"Why? To protect your legitimate claim to the name?"

Ben shook his head. "To do what's right. And I just think we all should know."

Keaton made a sound, not necessarily of agreement. "Right, then." He suddenly tossed back the entire contents of his drink and set the glass back down with decisiveness. "I'll help you look."

Watching the two men, so alike, even though they'd never once met, was incredibly strange.

In the end, Keaton Whitfield didn't linger long in the restaurant. Shortly after saying that he would help Ben in their search for any more of Gerald Robinson's children, he excused himself for the evening with the promise of remaining in touch with Ben.

"Well," Ella murmured after he left. "I guess there's no need for a DNA test in this instance." She half expected Ben to move around to the other side of the booth, but he didn't budge from his spot next to her.

"Nope." He toyed with his drink, his blue eyes seeming restless as they roved over her.

"It's probably weird, though. Coming face-to-face with a stranger who has your face?"

"There's always been someone who has my face," he said. "Wes." He looked toward the exit that Keaton had taken. "I never expected a third." He looked back down at his glass, his lips twisted. "And yeah. It's weird." He suddenly lifted his glass, holding it up. "We should be celebrating."

Ella lifted her wineglass and clinked it softly against his squat one. "Okay." She wasn't so sure Ben looked like he wanted to celebrate, though.

But he gestured to the waiter and ordered a bottle of champagne. "And keep them coming," he told him. "Plus we'll see the menu."

The waiter's expression perked up. Probably because of the expensive champagne Ben had requested. Maybe he was onto the scent of a profitable night on the job.

Ella didn't much care. It wouldn't have mattered to her if she and Ben were sitting in an unprepossessing café or the finest restaurant in the world.

She was with him.

They closed down the restaurant before Ben poured Ella into a cab that transported them back to their hotel. She didn't need Ben having to help her out of the cab when they got there to know she'd had way too much to drink, and she giggled when she stumbled against him. "These high heels are too high."

"You're too high on Cristal," he corrected with a chuckle, catching the coat she shed when they made their way through the very elegant, very British hotel lobby.

Ella pointed her finger at him. "You shouldn't have ordered so much of it, then." She turned her finger toward the call button for the elevator and sent him a smile. "It was like drinking stardust."

"Maybe that's why I ordered so much of it," he drawled. "So I could watch you drink stardust."

She smiled. "You're so darn pretty."

He let out a bark of laughter. "You're so drunk."

The elevator opened and she went inside. "Not so drunk I don't know what I'm doing." To prove it, she pressed the correct button for her floor. "See?"

He chuckled again and pulled off his own overcoat, draping it—along with hers—over his arm. "That proves it all right."

Ella sighed happily, turning in a slow twirl as she relived that moment with him in Harrods. When she stopped, she looked up into his face. "I feel like a princess."

He smiled indulgently. "You deserve to feel like a princess."

"I don't think you're going to need my help after tonight," she admitted.

His brows tugged together.

"Keaton said he'll help you find the others. I think he meant it."

"That doesn't mean I won't still need you."

She swayed a little as the elevator continued climbing, wishing his words meant something far more personal. "All the same." Before she thought better of it, she stretched up and pressed a kiss to his lean cheek. "Thank you for everything."

His head reared back like he'd been stung. "Ella—"

"Oh, stop worrying," she said huskily. "I'm not going to throw myself at you in the hotel elevator." She hugged her arms around herself and turned to face the elevator doors. "It might surprise you, but even after too much Cristal, I know when something is pointless."

"What am I going to do with you?" he muttered behind her.

"Nothing." The elevator stopped at her floor and the doors slid open. "Good night, Ben."

She stepped off the elevator car, only to feel his arm come around her waist and spin her around.

Off balance from the champagne they'd consumed and her unfamiliarly high shoes and *him*, she fell against him.

Then his mouth was on hers and his hand sank into her hair, gently tugging her head back. "Open your mouth, Ella."

Her lips parted.

He groaned and kissed her again, more deeply, shockingly deeply, and her inebriated senses jolted back into stark clarity. She breathlessly dragged her mouth from his. "Ben—"

He pressed her against the wall next to the door to her suite. "Say no, Ella, or don't say anything at all."

She slid her fingers wonderingly over his lips. "I don't want to say no."

His eyes darkened and he grabbed her hand, kissing her fingertips. "Where's your room key?"

She started to automatically answer, only to realize she didn't know. "I changed my clothes at Harrods. You'd already given them your credit card. I didn't think—"

He pulled her back into the elevator that was still hovering on her floor and jabbed the button for the floor above hers.

Her heart climbed up into her throat, then he was kissing her, and she didn't think anymore about room keys. All she thought about was him.

The elevator door opened again, and Ben took her hand, pulling her off and down the hallway to his room. He opened the door and hustled her inside, barely waiting for the door to shut behind them before he tossed their coats aside and spun her around again, this time facing away from him.

"All night I've been thinking about this," he murmured, kissing her shoulder as he reached for the long, heavy silver zipper that ran from collar to hem.

Ella shivered, feeling her dress loosen as he slowly pulled down the zipper. "H-have you?" It was an intoxicating thought.

"Haven't you?" The downward progress of the zipper slowed even more when it reached her waist. He drew his finger down her spine, stopping to expertly flick the clasp of her bra open before it continued lower, following the zipper down to the lace edge of her panties.

She exhaled audibly. She honestly hadn't thought about the zipper. She'd just liked the dress. Particularly because *he'd* liked the dress.

Now, she'd never think of zippers in the same way again.

Fortunately, he didn't seem to need an answer that she couldn't voice, anyway. Instead, he just pushed the dress forward from her shoulders along with her bra straps and it fell loosely down past her hips, sliding all the way to the floor with a soft rustle. Ben made a low sound, pushing her hair over her shoulder to kiss the nape of her neck. His warm hands clasped her hips, his fingertips slipping beneath the edge of her panties.

Ella's head fell forward like a broken flower on a stem. She could hardly breathe for the desire streaking through her.

"Tell me you're not a virgin," he murmured against the side of her neck.

"I'm not a virgin," she promised thickly. Though her previous experience paled almost comically in comparison. "I'm on the pill—"

He pushed her panties down her hips, dragging them slowly down her thighs. "Step out of them."

She stepped out of her shoes as well, then sucked in a sharp breath when he straightened again, drawing his hands slowly upward and inward over her naked skin. He was still fully clothed. "This doesn't strike me as fair," she said unevenly.

In answer, he moved around in front of her, clasped her waist and lifted her straight off the ground.

She gasped, instinctively winding her arms around him.

He carried her across his suite that she was dimly realizing eclipsed the size of hers and didn't set her down again until they were in the bedroom. Then he pulled her willing fingers to his tie.

Breathing hard, she slowly pulled the knot free, watching him in the soft light coming from the lamps on either side of the wide bed that had already been turned down.

When the tie hung loose around his neck, she went to work on the buttons of his shirt. She was divinely aware of the way his breath shortened when she made her way to his abdomen and she tugged the shirttails loose to finish the job. Then she slowly pushed the shirt off his shoulders and trailed her fingers over his chest, swirling in the unexpectedly silky hair that arrowed downward beneath his belt.

He caught her hand against his belly. "Sure you know what you're doing?"

She let out a soundless laugh. "No," she admitted, and undid his belt, anyway.

He groaned then, pushing her hand away to finish the job himself, kicking off his shoes at the same time. "You're killing me." He shucked the rest of his clothes in a smooth motion that spoke of experience she'd never ever possess, then he caught her against him and bore her down onto the mattress. But still he didn't take what she was so willing to give him.

And she was pretty sure she was the one who was dying. A person wasn't meant to experience such sensations and survive. She dragged her knee over his thigh, her fingers digging into the roping muscles of his shoulders, and she arched against him. "Please," she begged shamelessly. "Please, Ben—"

He covered her mouth with his again and sank into her.

She nearly bowed off the bed from the exquisite pleasure. She tore her mouth from his, gasping for breath against the hard, smooth skin of his neck.

Breathing harshly, he found her hands with his, pulled her arms above her head and twined his fingers through hers. "Are you okay?"

Tears were leaking from the corners of her eyes but she barely noticed. "Only if you never stop," she whispered.

He tightened his fingers against hers. "There's a thought," he said on a groan.

And then he said no more.

He just drove them both straight into a white-hot perfection from which Ella knew she'd emerge forever changed.

Chapter Fourteen

She woke to the sound of the shower running in the bathroom.

Flipping onto her back, Ella stared at the empty spot on the bed beside her. She ached in delicious places that longed for more.

What would he do if she joined him in the shower?

She clasped the velvety-smooth cotton sheet against her bare breasts and shifted restlessly. Making love with Ben was like nothing she'd ever imagined.

A faint buzzing penetrated and she realized Ben's cell phone was vibrating. The shower was still running. The nightstands were empty of everything except the highly polished lamp, and she slid out of bed, crouching to find Ben's trousers where they'd been half-kicked under the upholstered chair near glass French doors that offered a similar view of the park that her room possessed.

She flushed a little, thinking of the way his pants had come to be so carelessly treated and fished his cell phone out of a pocket. It had stopped vibrating, but the word *Bonita* was visible and she chewed her cheek for a moment. Finally, she snatched up the shirt Ben had been wearing the night before and pulled it over bare body. Then, since he'd left the bathroom door open, anyway, she carried the phone with her into the oversized room.

Across a sea of lavish marble, steam clouded the clear glass shower, but not so much so that the sight of him was entirely obscured and her stomach didn't hollow out.

She felt a sudden urge to turn tail and run. But her feet seemed incapable of movement.

And then he turned beneath the shower spray and saw her. He slowly pushed open the glass door and steam rolled out, billowing over the cool marble floor. "Ella?"

She couldn't seem to make her tongue form words and mutely held up his phone. "Ringing," she finally managed to say.

He slicked his hair back from his face. "Put the phone down."

She set it on the marble-topped white vanity beside her. "Come here."

Her feet unrooted themselves and she moved past the massive round tub toward the shower. Without stopping to shed his shirt that she wore, she joined him in the glass shower, feeling the sprays coming at her from all directions, not just above.

His eyes roved over her, taking in the shirt that was drenched in seconds and clinging to her body.

Then he tilted her chin with his finger and slowly—so slowly he stole her heart all over again—pressed his lips gently against hers.

Breath shuddered out of her. "Ben."

"Shhh." He began peeling the fine, nearly transparent

shirt away from her skin as if he was unwrapping the most precious of gifts. "Just let me," he whispered.

And she did.

They spent the afternoon exploring London.

Shockingly, Ben left his phone in his hotel suite. Not because he'd forgotten it, either. No, it had been a deliberate act.

And they did it her way.

No private drivers. No extravagance. They left all that behind at the hotel and went out on foot, armed with Ella's borrowed guidebook and an umbrella, even though the rain had stopped before they set out.

She wore the leather jacket he'd bought her the day before over her thermal shirt and jeans. He looked ridiculously sexy wearing his dark jeans with his long overcoat hanging from his shoulders and a pair of dark glasses perched on his nose.

They walked to Buckingham Palace, where Ella stared in awe through the gates at the massive building. "I wish it were open for tours this time of year."

It wasn't even fifty degrees out, but Ben felt warm inside. He looped his arm around Ella's shoulders and eyed the palace. "It's open during the summer for a few months, I think."

Maybe he'd bring Ella back.

The thought hit him like a punch to his solar plexus and Ella suddenly looked up at him, her eyes lighter than the pale blue sky overhead. "What?"

He shook his head. "Nothing. I caught the guard ceremony once. It was quite a spectacle."

She leaned more closely against his side. "I'll bet."

He looked around them. It was late January. There were still spectators like them, but the crowd was considerably smaller than what he'd seen on previous visits. "What's next in your guidebook?" They'd already spent half the day either sleeping or making love. And that meant there wasn't a lot of daylight left for them to explore in the manner Ella wanted.

She grinned and lifted the worn paperback. "Back to Hyde Park."

"Across from the hotel."

She nodded and they retraced their steps, heading into the park, where some patches of ice lurked on the paths. They stopped while Ella stared at the Diana Memorial Fountain, a great low loop of cascading water that was undoubtedly a star attraction on a hot day, and again when she insisted on purchasing them coffees from one of the kiosks they passed. She was clearly reveling in her exploration.

He'd seen it all before.

But even if he hadn't, he'd still just be reveling in her.

Aware of their limited time, they made their way to Kensington Gardens, where she stood and stared up at the Peter Pan statue, sipping her coffee, and made such a pretty picture he wished he had his phone just so he could have captured the moment on the camera he hadn't used since Stephanie took Henry away. They followed the many paths and viewed the statue of Queen Victoria against the backdrop of Kensington Palace. They didn't have enough time to properly tour the palace, but she browsed the gift shop, purchasing a small ornament for her mother, and then they bought sandwiches in the café there.

And then Ben had had enough walking and after leaving the palace and gardens behind, he hailed the first cab he spotted and even though he'd figured on having the cab take them around to more sights, Ella settled back against her seat and closed her eyes.

She was asleep in only minutes.

He took her gift-shop package before it dropped from

her lax fingers and told the driver to take them to their hotel instead, but to take his time. When they arrived, he paid the exorbitant fare and brushed his lips alongside her ear. "Come on, Sleeping Beauty. Time to wake up."

Her lashes lifted slowly and her full lips curved. "I was having the loveliest dream," she whispered. "We were in London."

He laughed softly and pulled her from the cab. "We are in London."

"Right." She pressed her hands against his chest and looked up at him through her lashes. "Thank you."

"For what?"

"Everything."

He didn't want to kiss her right there on the sidewalk outside the hotel. "Let's go up to my suite. You can finish your...nap."

The drowsiness in her eyes cleared slightly. "What are you suggesting, Mr. Robinson?"

He smoothed her long hair away from her creamy cheek. "Whatever gets you upstairs, Ms. Thomas."

She closed her eyes, smiling more widely. Then she fit her hand into his and led the way into the hotel. Once they were upstairs in his suite, she peeled off her leather jacket and gave him a look over her shoulder. "So far, that very lovely room of mine one floor down has gone almost entirely to waste."

"Got a complaint with the bed here?"

She pressed her lips together, her cheeks rosy.

"Didn't think so." He placed a kiss on her forehead and pulled her through the living area of the suite and into the larger of the two bedrooms it possessed.

She kicked off her tennis shoes and climbed onto the high, freshly made bed. "Naps are the best luxury in the world," she said, pulling one of the pillows close to her cheek and closing her eyes.

He waited a beat but she didn't move. "You're not really going to *nap*."

She lifted an eyelid, peering at him. Then she laughed. "Your expression," she said. "Classic." She suddenly rolled off the bed and went into the bathroom, closing the door behind her.

He raked his hands through his hair and absently noticed the message indicator on the phone next to the bed.

He could hear water running in the room next door and he picked up the phone to retrieve the message. It had been Keaton Whitfield, simply leaving his name and number.

Ben deleted the message and dialed the number, prowling around the room with the receiver at his ear.

A woman answered the line, serving to remind Ben that it was a workday, and after another series of clicks, Whitfield picked up.

"I wanted to apologize," the other man said. "For taking off so curtly last evening."

"I would've wanted to do the same thing." Ben sat on the edge of the bed, propping his elbows on his thighs, and cut to the chase. "Have you changed your mind about what you offered?"

"No." The other man was silent for a moment. "I wondered if you and your girlfriend were available for dinner this evening."

"Ella's not my girlfriend," Ben said abruptly. "She works for me."

"I mistook the situation. No matter. I'd still like to make up for last night."

A sound drew Ben's attention when Ella suddenly crossed the room, moving fast.

"Ella—"

She didn't wait.

And it dawned on him what he'd said. And that she'd overheard.

"It's my turn to be abrupt," he said into the phone. "I'll need to get back to you." He dropped the receiver on the cradle and went after Ella, only catching up to her because she got stuck in the hallway waiting for the elevator.

"Ella—"

She held out her hand, palm up. "Don't say anything."

"People don't shut me up."

Her jaw worked. She jabbed the call button for the elevator again, her fingers white-knuckle around the leather jacket she was clutching. "Sorry. I'm just an employee who doesn't know better."

"I didn't mean that."

She snorted and even though the elevator opened up beside her, she didn't get inside. She faced him, folding her arms defensively across her chest. "I'm not going to say I regret sleeping with you," she said tightly, seemingly oblivious to the gasp her words elicited from the elderly couple inside the elevator, "because it'd be a monumental lie. But it's not something that can continue. You don't do girlfriends. And I don't do—" her voice choked "—whatever this is."

Remorse sat heavy in his gut. "Ella."

She quickly slipped into the elevator just as the doors were closing again. He pressed the button, but the car was already going down.

He slammed his hand against the closed metal door and strode back into his suite, shoving the door closed behind him.

He looked down the length of the suite to the master bedroom at the end and saw Ella's tennis shoes lying on the floor at the foot of the bed.

He swore, mostly at himself.

Ella was twenty-three. Compared to the life he'd led, she was a babe in the woods. He was the one who was supposed to know better. To have some control.

To *not* be his father's son.

But what had he just done over the past twenty-four hours but prove how much like Gerald he still was?

They left London the next day. Ella had never retrieved her tennis shoes from him, and even though he'd intended to give them to her, when they left the hotel, she was already wearing the leather boots he'd bought for her at Harrods.

She had her nose buried in her textbook, clearly unwilling to talk, so he left the shoes untouched inside his garment bag.

When they were situated in their first-class seats once again, she lifted the partition that turned her seat into a private suite and she left it up nearly the entire time, only lowering it when she used the restroom or ordered a salad and tea several hours into the flight.

He wished he'd had an appetite for food.

He wished he'd had an appetite for anything other than Ella Thomas. Because if he had, she wouldn't be hurting now.

They landed in Austin and passed through customs without incident. A limo was waiting for them and Ben instructed the driver to let off Ella first. When the vehicle pulled up in front of her house, it was close to twelve hours since they'd left the ground in London.

It felt close to twelve days.

She didn't look at him as she gathered up her messenger bag while the driver carried her rolling suitcase to the front door of the house.

"Ella," he pleaded. "I never wanted to upset you."

"I know." She pursed her lips. In profile, her face looked young and pale. But that could have been attributed to the long flight and jet lag. "I told you I was a big girl, Ben. Let's just chalk it up to being out of the country and get back to normal." She pushed open the door without waiting for the driver to do it for her. "No harm, no foul, right?"

She pushed the door closed on him before he could respond.

Not that he had a suitable response, anyway.

"Wait until she gets inside," he said through the intercom when the driver returned to the car.

"Yes, sir."

Through the tinted window beside him, he watched Ella march up the ramp. She grabbed hold of the suitcase and disappeared through the front door.

She didn't look back.

"Okay to go now, sir?" The driver's disembodied voice spoke to him.

He realized he was rubbing the center of his hollow chest and dropped his hand. "Yes."

The limo pulled away from Ella's house and Ben closed his eyes. He hoped it wasn't going to be too long before he could do so without seeing her image smiling winsomely up at him.

When he let himself into his own house a short while later, Mrs. Stone appeared, looking typically grim. "Clear out Henry's room," he said abruptly. "Give all the stuff away to a shelter or something."

She actually showed some expression of surprise. "Are you sure, Mister? What about the photograph in your room?"

"Yes, I'm sure. He's not coming back," he said flatly, and strode up the stairs toward his office. He was almost at the top when he spoke again. "Mrs. Stone. Keep the picture."

In his office, he placed Ella's tennis shoes on the center of his desk, where she'd find them when she showed up for work.

Only she didn't.
Not the next day.

Or the next.

It was only at the end of the week, when he was weeding through the pile of message slips that Bonita had left, that he found the one from Rosa at Spare Parts. The temporary agency he'd used to find Ella in the first place.

He shoved aside the rest of the messages, not caring the way they scattered, and called Rosa at the agency.

"Oh, Mr. Robinson." She sounded relieved. "I was hoping you'd return my call. As I relayed earlier, regrettably, Ms. Thomas wasn't able to complete her assignment with you because of a personal matter. But I have a few other candidates I think might be suitable, if you'd like me to send them around."

His only interest in Spare Parts had been Ella.

It didn't take a stretch to know that he was the personal matter preventing her from returning. "No, thank you, Rosa. My needs have changed."

"Of course. Please don't hesitate to contact me in the future if—"

"I will," he interrupted. "Good night." He disconnected and turned his chair around to stare out the windows behind his desk. "You've only got yourself to blame," he said.

"Talking to yourself is the first sign."

He swiveled around again to see Wes. "First sign of what?"

"The insanity of being a Robinson." Wes threw himself down into one of the chairs fronting Ben's desk and stretched. "So I'm here—" he glanced at his watch "—at eight at night, as requested by the esteemed Bonita. Question is why?"

"That's something we'd like to know, too," Zoe said, entering the office with the rest of their sisters on her heels. "Rachel had to have Matteo fly her in from Horseback Hollow, for goodness sake."

Rachel looked less perturbed than Zoe did about this

fact. Probably because she rightfully sensed the point of the meeting was about their father. And Zoe had a blind eye where Gerald was concerned.

"I doubt Matteo minds too much," he said drily. It gave his sister's husband an opportunity to visit his brother Joaquin, who'd been consulting on Robinson Tech's recent expansion and rebranding.

Zoe rolled her eyes, not at all pacified.

Kieran and Graham brought up the rear and dragged chairs around from the conference table on the other side of Ben's office so there were enough places to sit.

"Maybe meeting at your house would have been better," Rachel said, moving to look out his office door. "You're sure Dad isn't going to walk in us or something?"

"Maybe he should," Zoe muttered.

"Bonita assures me that he and Mother are at a charity banquet this evening," Ben said. He leaned back in his seat, bouncing the end of his pen against his desk. Then he tossed it aside and sat forward. "We have a brother," he said bluntly. His eyes met Wes's for a moment.

"We have lots of brothers," Sophie pointed out wryly.

"Another one," Wes offered before Ben could.

"Yeah. His name's Keaton Whitfield. He lives in London."

"So that's what that sudden trip of yours was about," Graham said. Instead of sitting, he'd chosen to lean against the window near the conference table. He was only two years younger than Ben and Wes, and if anyone could be considered the peacemaker of the family, it was him.

Maybe because he'd been smart enough to choose cattle over computers.

"Ella found him." Just saying her name made that hollow feeling in his chest show up again, and he yanked his tie loose, wanting to alleviate the discomfort.

"How do you know he's not lying?" Zoe challenged, arching a smooth brow.

"He looks like us," Ben said, meeting Wes's gaze again. "Trust me. There's no doubt."

Wes's lips twisted and he looked down at his hands clasped across his stomach.

Rachel perched forward on her chair. At twenty-seven, she was the oldest of his sisters. And though she wasn't quite as opposed to Ben's hunt for Gerald's illegitimate offspring, she was much more interested in his Fortune beginnings. "What about Kate Fortune?"

"Still in the hospital, last I checked."

"What about our grandmother? Have you found out anything more about Jacqueline Fortune?"

He shook his head. "Ella—" Dammit. He pushed out of his chair. "We haven't been able to find out if she's actually dead or not. There's something weird going on there."

"You're suspicious about everything." Olivia spoke for the first time. "You have been ever since that witch took Henry—" She broke off when Ben pinned her with a glare. "What?" She looked around for support. "We're all thinking it."

Wes pinched the bridge of his nose before standing. "I've got a dating app to roll out in a few weeks," he said. "Unless you've got anything else I need to know, I'm out of here."

"Keaton said he'd help us find the others," Ben stated.

Wes's lips twisted. "Happy day." He left the office, closing the door after himself again.

Zoe moved to take his seat. "What do you hope to accomplish?" she demanded. "If you *do* find this Jacqueline person?"

"I don't know," Ben admitted, suddenly weary of the entire matter. The fact that it was an unexpected response was clear in the expressions looking back at him.

He wished he could leave the same way Wes had, but he'd been the one to call the meeting in the first place. He sat back in his chair, spreading his hands, palms upward on the desktop. "I started out wanting to drag our father's indiscretions out into the light. So I'd feel better about myself, I guess." The admission was hard.

"Oh, Ben," Rachel murmured.

"Don't say I'm not like him," he returned. "My whole life I've been told how much I'm like him. Stephanie showing up with the baby when she did—" He looked at Rachel. "I felt like a chip right off the old block."

"You started out," Graham prompted. "Does that mean something's changed?"

"Not the end result," Ben admitted. "I looked at Keaton earlier this week and I…I *want* to know if there are more of us out there. More people we have a connection with. More people our father has let down in ways we can't even begin to understand."

"To what?" Zoe looked skeptical. "To *help* them?"

He thought of Randy Phillips, with whom Bonita had already scheduled an on-site visit. "Whitfield doesn't need our help. He's successful in his own right. But what if there are others? Struggling or—"

"I always knew you were a softy," Rachel murmured. She got out of her seat and gave Ben a kiss on the cheek, never knowing the sting that her words carried.

In Boston, Ella had accused him of being a softy. He'd done a bang-up job of showing her otherwise.

If he hadn't, maybe she'd have still been in his life.

But they were done. His actions had seen to that.

When the rest of his brothers and sisters had finally left him alone in his office, he pulled out his cell phone and pulled up the data for his personal bank account.

With a few more taps of his fingertips, he issued the

compensation they'd agreed on to be mailed to her home. She'd have a check in a few days at the latest.

Then he pocketed his phone and walked to his office door. "Now we're done," he said, and snapped off the light.

Chapter Fifteen

Only they weren't done.

Because three days later, Ben was staring in disbelief at the envelope he'd just opened.

The check he'd issued to Ella was inside. Ripped cleanly in half.

"Bonita," he yelled, but didn't wait for his secretary to haul herself into his office. He went to her and shook the envelope at her. "When did this arrive?"

She gave him a mild look over her reading glasses. "Do you need more prunes in your diet, Ben? You seem awfully constipated since you returned from London last week."

He slapped the envelope down on her tidy desk. "There's no stamp on it. Was it hand-delivered?"

She raised her eyebrows. "How would I know that?" Being the know-it-all that she always was, she plucked out the two halves of the check and studied them. "Well, that's quite a sum of money," she murmured.

He stormed back into his office, slamming the door after himself.

He crossed the office and dialed Ella's home number. But it just rang and rang, not even being picked up by an answering machine.

He strode back out of his office. "I'm going out," he told Bonita.

"You have a departmental meeting in a half hour."

His steps didn't slow. He was fueled by a fury that he'd never before felt. "Cancel it. Or handle it yourself. At the moment, I don't much give a damn."

It was probably a miracle that he didn't get stopped for speeding when he drove to Ella's house. He pulled the Porsche up into their cracked driveway and, not giving himself a chance to think, darted up the ramp and knocked hard on the door.

"They're not there," a voice said from behind him, and Ben whirled to see a wizened old man standing on the other side of the bushes separating the driveways.

Ben approached the hedge. "Where are they?"

"The hospital, o' course." The man gestured with his hedge trimmers. "You're that fancy fella Ella knows."

Ben didn't feel fancy. Fear tore through him so violently, he felt like shredding the hedge with his bare hands. "What hospital? What for? What happened?"

"Rory." The other man's eyes squinted. "University. Kid got himself another case of pneumonia."

Ben yanked out his phone and called Bonita. "Find out the status of Rory Thomas," he barked. "Patient at University Brackenridge. Call me back." He hung up on the sound of her railing at him and looked back at the old man. "How long ago did he get sick?"

He scratched the white whiskers that sparsely populated his wrinkled cheeks. "Sometime last week. My memory's not so good sometimes."

"Thank you." Ben suddenly reached across the hedge to shake the old man's hand.

"Bernie," the man said, and wiped his palm on his shirt before shaking Ben's hand. "That's some car you got," he called when Ben returned to the Porsche. "But you slow your butt down 'cause there's kids in this neighborhood!"

Difficult as it was, Ben moderated his speed. At least until he hit the highway. He reached the hospital in record time and called Bonita again when he pulled into the parking structure. "Well?"

"Cool your jets or I'm going to give myself a well-deserved raise," she said tartly. "It's not that easy getting information about a patient, you know. There are such things as privacy rules and—"

"Do you have a room number or not?"

She sighed mightily and gave him one.

"It's not ICU or anything, is it?"

"Not that I know of."

It was good enough for him and he breathed a little easier. "Thanks."

He left the parking garage and made his way through the hospital, taking a detour when he spotted the gift shop on his way. He didn't know what the heck to purchase for a teenage boy. And he left the gift shop again with a bouquet of bobbing red and yellow balloons that made him feel more than a little self-conscious, a bag full of junk food that no doctor would allow a pneumonia patient to consume and a chess set.

When he finally found his way to Rory's room, the door was ajar and he knocked lightly with his balloon hand.

The door swung open wider, and Elaine Thomas looked up from her position sitting next to the hospital bed.

Her lips parted a little at the sight of him, and then she set aside the book she'd been reading and gestured for him to enter. "Rory, look who's here."

Never feeling less certain in his life, Ben looked at the boy in the bed. But Rory didn't look all that different than he had after the chess tournament. Maybe a little paler.

Definitely not as pale as his sister looked.

Ella was sitting on the other side of the bed in front of the window and she was whiter than Rory's bedsheets, her hair looking like fire as it streamed loose around her shoulders.

He didn't look at her, though. Because if he did, the emotion in him would take hold again.

Instead, he kept his focus on Rory and the boy's mom, lifting his weird collection of gifts. "I didn't know what to bring," he admitted.

Elaine quickly unwrapped the ribbons holding the balloons from his hand and attached them to the foot of Rory's bed. "It's very sweet of you," she said, giving Rory a look.

"Yeah." The kid was obviously more interested in the chess set, and the bag of candy bars and sweets that Ben handed him than he was the balloons. "Thanks." He set the chess box on the rolling table beside his bed and peered into the plastic bag. "Oh, nice," he breathed. "Peanut butter cups."

"I didn't know you'd gotten sick," Ben said. "I would have—"

Ella's chair suddenly screeched against the floor and she stepped around him, leaving the room.

"—come sooner," Ben admitted.

"Perhaps you should go after her," Elaine suggested.

Ben's chest felt tight. "And say what?"

"Say what's in your heart."

"I've never once been told to do that." The admission came out of nowhere. "Maybe I don't know how."

But Elaine didn't look shocked. "Have you ever once looked at a woman the way I see you look at my daughter?" She smiled gently. "You'll know how when the time comes."

Ben needed no more urging.

He followed Ella out into the corridor, where she was pacing back and forth, flags of color now flying in her cheeks.

Her eyes snapped as he approached her. "You shouldn't have come."

"Why not? We had an agreement," he said. "Remember? You help my search and in return I pay—"

"The agreement changed," she cut him off, her voice tight. "You think I don't know how much you paid for me to go to Boston? To *London*? The hotels? The clothes? Everything? I can't return those things. But I certainly didn't need that check you sent!" She looked defensive. "I don't know if you meant it for services rendered or just more charity—"

He grabbed her arms and hauled her close to his face. "Shut. Up."

She looked outraged. "I don't take orders from you, Ben Robinson."

"No, but you'll sneak off with my heart," he snapped, and let her go again, moving across the corridor, because he was either going to shake her or kiss her.

Doing the former was against everything he believed, and doing the latter was what had gotten him in over his head with her in the first place.

Ella shook her head, trying to clear it of the odd buzzing inside. She obviously hadn't heard him correctly because Ben believed he didn't have a heart. "You made it plain I couldn't continue working for you—"

"When the *hell* did I do that?"

A nurse walking down the hall on squeaky shoes gave them a censorious look.

Ella raked back her loose hair with shaking hands. Since she'd returned from London only to discover Rory had gotten sick again, she'd practically been living at the hospital. She and her mom traded off nights spent there so Rory would never be alone.

She still felt guilty for being in London. Walking through parks with Ben. Lying in bed with Ben. Losing her heart to Ben. All while her brother had been home, stricken with yet another case of pneumonia.

"You held up your end of our agreement," Ben's gruff voice broke the silence. "Just because I couldn't keep my hands off you doesn't change anything. You found Keaton Whitfield. You earned every cent."

"I don't *want* your money!"

"Not even for the security it offers?"

"I told you before that security based on anything other than truth is nothing at all."

His eyes went dark. "You think I'm lying to you?"

"I think your conscience works overtime trying not to be like your father," she said thickly. "But you don't have to pay me off."

"If you say something like that one more time, I'm not going to be responsible for what I do." His voice turned flat. "You brought the check to my office. Didn't you."

She swallowed, wishing she'd just stuck a postage stamp on the envelope and mailed the check back to him. Or that she'd torn it up and thrown it in the trash.

She still wasn't sure what insanity had driven her to Robinson Tech.

"I left it with the girl at the reception desk."

"So you threw it in my face from a safe distance."

She couldn't deny what was true. "You mailed the thing to me in the first place!" She pushed the reminder through her tight throat. "I didn't take it up to your office because I didn't want to do this." She waved her hands.

"Do this." His jaw worked and she finally noticed the loose tie and the tired lines around his eyes and the five o'clock shadow that he'd only let show once when they'd flown to London.

Even his hair looked disheveled. As if his fingers had been raking through it.

"Deal with me in person," he said in a flat tone. "That's what you mean?"

"I can't think straight when you're here in person!"

"That makes two of us, then." He turned and walked away.

Ella wrapped her arms around her stomach and leaned back against the wall for support. If she collapsed, she'd probably end up hauled into a hospital room of her own.

But he only went about ten paces before he stopped. "No," she heard him say. "No, this is *not* how this works."

Then he wheeled around and came back to her, not stopping until the toes of his shoes were touching the toes of hers.

His gaze bore into hers and when she tried to look away, he caught her chin in his hand. "Look at me."

She couldn't bear it. "Why can't you ever let anything go, Ben?" She knew it sounded strange when they'd only known each other a month, but she felt like they'd packed a lifetime in the whirlwind of those days. "You're holding on to Henry's room like it was a shrine. You're holding on to your father's sins like they were your own. You're—" His thumb pressed over her lips, cutting off the words.

"I'm my father's son," he said gruffly.

Tears burned behind her eyes. "You're not anyone but you." She let out a choked laugh entirely devoid of humor. "The man who doesn't do normal stuff. Like girlfriends."

"Is that what you want?" His voice was low. "To be my girlfriend?"

She trembled. She wanted so much more than that. "You don't even want to work with me."

He started to swear again, only to bite it off when that same nurse passed them by with her squeaky, rubber-soled shoes and looks of disapproval. His teeth visibly clenched, then he exhaled deeply. "When did I ever tell you that?"

"You didn't have to. Your actions—"

"*What* actions?" He took a step back and threw out his arms. "You got on the plane in London not talking to me. Okay, I get that one," he admitted quickly. "You heard what I said to Keaton. But what the hell did you expect me to say to him? I've never kissed and told, even when I didn't give a flying fig about the one I was kissing.

"Should I have told the guy who we'd just learned was walking, talking, living proof that my father was as bad as I'd ever feared that I'd just spent the best hours of my life with you? A girl he knew *worked* for me? A girl who deserved protection from guys like me?"

Ella blinked, and the stinging behind her eyes worsened. "Best hours?"

But Ben wasn't listening. "You got off the plane from London and decimated me without so much as a blink of your blue eyes. 'No harm, no foul,'" he said, quoting her. "You made sure I knew what happened over there hadn't mattered to you. It was just all part of the experience."

He pressed his fingertip against her chest, squarely between her breasts, where her heart was pounding. "*You* finished things between us, Ella. *You* made sure I knew you weren't coming back even before I got that call from Spare Parts." He yanked his hand back and shoved both fists into his pockets. "All I did was close the checkbook on my end of the deal. Because I thought it was right. And fair. But you— You obviously think otherwise."

"It did matter to me," she whispered. "What happened meant everything. You meant everything."

He shook his head, looking down at the floor. "You didn't tell me about Rory getting sick. If I'd known—"

She blinked, but her vision wouldn't clear. There were too many tears trying to get free. "You'd have what? Called the president this time to make sure my brother got the best care possible?"

He looked at her. "I'd have been here with you."

A breath shuddered out of her. The tears escaped, sliding down her face. She wiped her nose inelegantly on the long sleeve of her thermal shirt.

He slowly moved toward her again. Until the toes of his shoes were once more against the toes of hers.

And this time, he lowered his forehead until it rested against hers. "I don't do girlfriends, Ella, because I've never known how before. The only place where I've ever succeeded was in business. So imagine, if you would, what I'm contending with when it comes to you."

Her breath was jerking unevenly through her. "I don't know what that means."

"It means I can't seem to get through the day without a pain here." He grabbed her palm and flattened it against his chest. "Just because you aren't with me. It means I want what we had in London. And more. And if I haven't ever successfully navigated having a *girlfriend*, how much worse would I be at having a wife?"

Everything—breathing, shaking, crying—stilled. She wasn't sure if maybe the world hadn't stopped moving, too. She looked up at him.

"Somewhere between walking a snowy Boston street with you and watching you twirl around in a London elevator, I fell in love with you," he said roughly. "And thanks to my mother and father, I've got one of the worst examples of marriage to learn from. But even knowing *that* isn't enough to stop me from wanting to marry you."

The earth spun again in a dizzying rush. Her tears fell even faster. "Ben."

He slid his hand into her hair, tangling his fingers in it. "I'm the worst sort of risk for a girl who wants security."

"Maybe a girl who wanted security is exactly the sort of risk you need." She wrapped her hands around his neck, rubbing her thumbs slowly over his bristly jaw. "I'm sorry. I'm so sorry. I didn't know I could hurt you."

His fingers tightened in her hair. "I don't want your apologies. I just want you."

"You have me. You've always had me." She went up on her toes and brushed her lips against his. "I don't need money for security. I just need to know you love me as much as I love you."

He caught her wrists in his hands and pulled them from his neck. But only to press his lips to her knuckles. "You'll marry me."

She smiled through her tears. "Is there a question mark at the end of that demand?"

He looked at her over their clasped hands. "What do you think?"

Warmth spread through her, feeling like the sun was hitting after she'd feared she'd never feel it again.

In turn, she pressed her lips to his knuckles. "Yes."

"Yes, it was a question mark, or yes, you'll marry me?"

She felt the smile stretching her lips. "What do you think?"

He exhaled and dragged her closer. "I think my entire life has been on hold, waiting for you to come into it."

Fresh tears flooded her eyes. "Yes, I'll marry you."

"When?"

She threw her head back and suddenly laughed. Because some things might have changed where Ben Robinson was concerned, but his constant forward motion wasn't one of them. "As soon as Rory's out of the hospital."

He swore softly. "I didn't even think. Is he doing okay? I didn't know how bad off—"

"It's his third case of pneumonia," she said. "But he's on the mend. The doctors are keeping him for a few more days to be extracautious. We expect he'll be released early next week."

"What does he need?"

"For you to stop making out with his sister in the hall outside his door!"

They both looked over to see her brother standing with his crutches in the doorway to his room. He was looking disgusted and pleased all at the same time. Elaine, who was standing beside her son, looked weepy.

And in that moment, Ben wrote off any notion he had of hustling Ella off to the nearest justice of the peace. He wasn't marrying into a family who did things as expediently as possible.

"I'm marrying your sister," he told Rory. "That okay with you?"

Rory grimaced. "No accounting for taste. She's pretty bossy most of the time." Then he grinned slyly. "You could sweeten the deal with that new OS Robinson Tech's coming out with."

Ben's laugh barked out of him. "Rory, you can have the first copy of the new operating system as soon as testing's finished. First, you've got to get yourself well enough to get out of this place so you can give away your sister at our wedding."

"When's *that* going to be?"

"If you're out of here next week, I don't know. Maybe Valentine's Day?"

Ella gaped at him. "That's only a few weeks away! Can we really put together a wedding that fast?"

"Your father and I planned our wedding in two weeks,"

Elaine said. She was smiling slightly. "Where there's a will, there's a way."

Ben looked down at Ella. "I'd marry you tomorrow, but if you need more time, I'll wait. As long as it takes, I'll wait. But in the meantime, I'm calling my jeweler. He can bring engagement rings here. You can pick out whatever—"

She pressed her fingers over his lips, silencing him. "I don't want to wait to marry you," she whispered. "To plan some elaborate, fancy wedding. If you want me to have an engagement ring, that's fine, but the ring that matters most is the wedding ring you'll slide on my finger. I want to be your *wife*. The sooner the better." She slid her arm around his back and pressed her cheek against his shoulder. "Go back in your room, Rory."

"See? Bossy." But the kid was grinning when he turned and disappeared into his room again.

And that left Elaine standing there.

"I'll take care of your daughter, Mrs. Thomas," he promised. "She'll never want for anything."

"Call me Elaine. And as long as Ella never wants for love, she'll have all that I've ever hoped." Then she, too, turned and disappeared inside the hospital room, but this time, she closed the door with a soft click.

Ben turned back to Ella and he gently wiped his thumbs over her wet cheeks. "You'll never want for my love," he promised gruffly. "I never thought those words would ever come out of my mouth."

Her translucent eyes shimmered. "Another first. A good one?"

"The best." He kissed her softly.

Until he heard the ominous squeak of those nurse's shoes again and he looked up to see the testy-looking woman with her hands propped on her generous hips. "You're not planning to start your honeymoon right here on my ward, are you?" she asked.

Ella let out a gasping laugh that she tried to bury against his shoulder.

But then the nurse gave him a quick, wholly unexpected wink. "Room 509," she said. "Empty. Might want to give it a try."

And she turned on her squeaky soles and sashayed away.

* * * * *

Don't miss the next installment of the new Harlequin Special Edition continuity

THE FORTUNES OF TEXAS: ALL FORTUNE'S CHILDREN

Vivian Blair thinks that passion is overrated—and that her new app is the ideal way to find the perfect partner. Until she falls head over heels for her boss, Wes Robinson—the one man with whom she's got nothing in common!

Look for
FORTUNE'S PERFECT VALENTINE
by
USA TODAY *bestselling author Stella Bagwell*
On sale February 2016, wherever
Harlequin books are sold.

COMING NEXT MONTH FROM

H HARLEQUIN®

SPECIAL EDITION

Available January 19, 2016

#2455 FORTUNE'S PERFECT VALENTINE
The Fortunes of Texas: All Fortune's Children • by Stella Bagwell
Computer programmer Vivian Blair believes the secret to a successful marriage is
compatibility, while her boss, Wes Robinson, thinks passion's the only ingredient in
a romance. When she develops a matchmaking app and challenges him to use it,
which one will prove the other right...and find true love?

#2456 DR. FORGET-ME-NOT
Matchmaking Mamas • by Marie Ferrarella
When Dr. Mitchell Stewart begins volunteering at a shelter alongside teacher
Melanie McAdams, he falls head-over-stethoscope for the blonde beauty. Once
burned in love, Melanie's not looking for forever, even in the capable arms of a man
like Mitchell. Can the medic's bedside manner convince Melanie to open her heart
to a happy ending?

#2457 A SOLDIER'S PROMISE
Wed in the West • by Karen Templeton
Former soldier Levi Talbot returns to Whispering Pines, New Mexico, to make
good on his promise to look after his best friend's family. The last thing he expects
is to fall in love with his pal's widow, Valerie Lopez. Now, Levi's in for the battle of
his life—one he's determined to win.

#2458 THE DOCTOR'S VALENTINE DARE
Rx for Love • by Cindy Kirk
Dr. Noah Anson's can-do attitude has always met with success, both
professionally and personally. But when he runs up against the most stubborn
woman in Jackson Hole, Josie Campbell, nothing goes the way he planned. It
will take a whole lotta lovin' to win Josie's heart...and that's what he's
determined to do!

#2459 WAKING UP WED
Sugar Falls, Idaho • by Christy Jeffries
When old friends Kylie Chatterson and Drew Gregson wake up in Las Vegas with
matching wedding bands, all they want to say is "I don't!" But when they're forced
to live together and care for Drew's twin nephews, they realize married life might
be the happy ending they'd both always dreamed of.

#2460 A VALENTINE FOR THE VETERINARIAN
Paradise Animal Clinic • by Katie Meyer
Single mom and veterinarian Cassie Marshall swore off men for good when her ex
walked out on her. But Alex Santiago, new to Paradise and its police department,
and his adorable K9 partner melt Cassie's heart. This Valentine's Day, can the doc
and the deputy create a forever family?

**YOU CAN FIND MORE INFORMATION ON UPCOMING HARLEQUIN® TITLES,
FREE EXCERPTS AND MORE AT WWW.HARLEQUIN.COM.**

HSECNM0116

SPECIAL EXCERPT FROM

HARLEQUIN

SPECIAL EDITION

*Dr. Mitchell Stewart experiences unusual symptoms
when he meets beautiful volunteer Melanie McAdams.
His heart's pounding and his pulse is racing...could this
be love? But it'll take some work to show commitment-
shy Melanie he means forever...*

*Read on for a sneak preview of
DR. FORGET-ME-NOT, the latest volume in*
Marie Ferrarella's
MATCHMAKING MAMAS miniseries.

Closing her eyes for a moment, Melanie sighed. She had
no answer for the taunting voice in her head. No theory
to put forth to satisfy her conscience and this sudden,
unannounced huge wave of guilt that had just washed
over her like a tsunami after a 9.9 earthquake. And, like
it or not, that was what Mitch's kiss had felt like to her,
an earthquake. A great, big, giant earthquake and she
wasn't even sure if the ground beneath her feet hadn't
disappeared altogether, thanks to liquefaction. She felt
just that unsteady.

   She'd stayed sitting down even after Mitch had left
the room.

   *Damn it, the man kissed you. He didn't perform a
lobotomy on you with his tongue. Get a grip and get back
to work. Life goes on, remember?*

   That was just the problem. Life went on. The love
of her life had been taken away ten months ago and for
some reason, life still went on.

Squaring her shoulders, she slid off the makeshift exam table, otherwise known in her mind as the scene of the crime, tested the steadiness of her legs and, once that was established, left the room.

Whether Melanie liked it or not, there was still a lot of work to do, and it wasn't going to get done by itself.

She had almost managed to talk herself into a neutral, rational place as she made her way past the dining hall, which, when Mitch was here, still served as his unofficial waiting room. That was when she heard Mitch call out to her.

"Melanie, I need you."

Everything inside her completely froze.

It was the same outside. It was as if her legs, after working fine all these years, had suddenly forgotten how to move and take her from point A to point B.

She had to have heard him wrong.

The Dr. Mitchell Stewart she had come to know these past few weeks would have never uttered those words to anyone, least of all to her.

And would the Mitchell Stewart you think you know so well have singed off your lips like that?

Turn your love of reading into rewards you'll love with
Harlequin My Rewards

MYR16R

Love the Harlequin book you just read?

Your opinion matters.

Review this book on your favorite book site, review site, blog or your own social media properties and share your opinion with other readers!